The Big Stinky City

Jason Deas

Ball Ground, Georgia, USA

3-Day Ranch Press

© 2012

Cover Design: Josh Merriam

This book is dedicated to:

Monique Krulick (Ma Tante Monique)

I barely know where to start in thanking you for your tireless and selfless work editing this novel. I will never forget your generosity. I look forward to hearing your laugh, in person, sometime soon.

"Always be a first-rate version of yourself, instead of a second-rate version of somebody else."

Judy Garland

Part I

Chapter 1

Believe it or not my name is Mash. My older brother Cecil wanted Mama to call me Mashed Potato, and she met him halfway and just called me Mash. We live in a big stinky city. We are surrounded by a zillion people, and there is noise at all hours of the day and night. Sometimes I wonder what it is like to hear nothing.

I live with my grandma, my mama, and Cecil whom I already told you about. I have no idea where my granddad and daddy are. We don't talk about them around here. If you try to talk about them you get yelled at and sometimes you might hear cussing and see somebody throw something across the room.

We live on the thirteenth floor of a twenty-seven floor building. Cecil is fifteen and I am eleven. I don't know how old my mama is, and if you ask grandma, she will tell you that she lies about her age, so it doesn't do any good asking. She asked me to guess one time and when I did, she just laughed and laughed at the number I said.

I have a brown face. My arms are brown and so are my legs. Pretty much all of me is brown. People call me black—whatever. Mama insists on being called African-American. I don't care too much about color like some people do. I care about what you have inside. Call me what you will.

My best friend lives on the fifth floor of my building, and his name is Charles. He has a mama *and* a daddy. Sometimes I pretend his daddy is my daddy too. Charles's daddy works all the time as a bus mechanic, but when he is home, he pays Charles a lot of attention. He doesn't drink like a lot of the other men in our building, and he even goes to church with us sometimes when the Atlanta Falcons aren't playing.

I want to be a pilot when I grow up. Planes fly over our place all the time, and I can't help but wonder every time I see one where it is going. I always wish I was sitting in one of the seats on the planes getting away from here. I dream of where the planes might be going and what the people on them might be doing. Cecil says I'm dumb for thinking this way. He says people like us don't grow up to be anything more than working stiffs. As soon as he said that, I decided not to believe him. My teacher, Ms. Monique, told me I could be anything I wanted to be, and I choose to believe her. I am going to be a pilot.

Today is Thursday morning; the month is February. Five inches of snow fell last night, and for Atlanta, Georgia, that is a strange thing. School is canceled for the day, and mama told me to go out and play. In her language, that means she has something private to do in the house, and I should not come back for at least two hours. Grandma is probably at the library. I'd be surprised if she hasn't read every book in there yet. Cecil doesn't go to school too often anyway, so this is just another day for him. For me... I'm going on an adventure—I'm going to be a pilot one day for crying out loud.

Chapter 2

Across the street from my building is another building that I can hardly believe is still standing. A restaurant. It is a midget among giants. It is one of the only one story buildings I have ever seen in person. The building is owned by Mr. Henry Johnson; he goes by Mr. Henry. Here is how the story goes, and I don't know how much of it is true. Mr. Henry's daddy was a strong minded man. He had a lot of enemies and a lot of friends as well. He was the first land owner in his line, and he purchased a quarter of an acre with hard earned dollars. The city was small at that point. Nobody knew this land would be worth millions in the future. When the future came and the city tried to buy his land, Mr. Henry's daddy, with the help of friends and guts and lawyers, kept his land. Some people said he could have been a millionaire. He said he didn't care.

His restaurant is called Hog's. It has the world's greatest egg sandwich. My mama has never bought me one but I've had plenty. I work for my meals. Mr. Henry does not believe in charity. Sometimes I wash dishes, and sometimes I scrub floors. Sometimes I get an easy job like filling up all the salt and pepper shakers. One day when I did a real good job he gave me an egg sandwich, fried potatoes and a dollar bill. I am so proud of that dollar. I still have it—I never spent it. I respect it too much to part with it.

This morning, Mr. Henry needs the snow shoveled from the front sidewalk so people won't slip coming in. People must have their egg sandwich, rain or shine. Shovel it, and they will come. I have never handled a snow shovel, and Mr. Henry laughs as he tells me it really isn't a snow shovel but a flat-nosed shovel. He says there *is* a difference. He says him owning a snow shovel would be like me owning a pair of water skis. As I throw the snow off the sidewalk, I get it.

When I finish the sidewalk there is a hot cup of cocoa waiting for me at the counter. As I hop up on the stool, Mr. Henry winks at me and asks me if I want the usual. I nod my head at him and he goes to work cooking. Judd, an older friend I've made from a tattoo parlor in town, sits down next to me.

"Let me guess," he says, smiling, "you're having an egg sandwich?"

"Yep," I say. Judd is older than I am, but not old enough to call sir, yet. "I shoveled the walk."

"I thought you might have," Judd says. "Come and do some work for me and I'll give you a free tattoo."

This is one of Judd's favorite jokes. I bet he has said it to me at least ten times, if not more. "You know my mama would kill me." I answer the same way every time and he laughs like it was the first.

"You got time to hand out some papers?" he asks. "Maybe people will have the day off and get a tat today."

Every now and then I walk up and down the street and hand out little sheets of paper advertising Judd's tattoo parlor. It is called Art Inkorporated. Judd isn't the owner of the shop, but I think he is the most talented artist that works there. Two other people work in the shop. A girl, named Gina, who has earrings in her nose and eyebrow and even one in her lip. I keep wanting to ask her how she blows her nose and if boogers get all caught up in it, but I don't know her well enough for this type of question. The owner is a guy named Paul. He has a beard like a Billy goat and tattoos of skeletons and scary stuff all over his arms and legs.

"I need to ask Mr. Henry if he has any more work for me," I tell Judd, "and if he doesn't, I can help you out for sure."

A minute later, Mr. Henry sets my plate in front of me. The plate is full. Not only does it have an egg sandwich on it, but it also has fried potatoes and grits. I look up at Mr. Henry and he gives me a giant smile.

"You earned it, Mash," he says. "It's cold out there and most kids wouldn't come out looking for work in this weather like you did."

"Thank you, Mr. Henry. Is there anything else I can do for you after I eat?"

"No, the walk looks great."

"OK. Judd needs my help with something, but I wanted to ask you first."

"Could you stop by before the lunch rush to see if the walk needs another shovel?" Mr. Henry asks.

"Yes, sir," I answer.

Mama always taught me to say sir and ma'am. I can't remember ever not saying it to her and grandma. I say it to Charles's daddy and mama, Ms. Monique, Mr. Henry, all the older folks at church and school. It's almost like magic words. When you give somebody respect, most times they give it right back. Whenever I meet somebody new, as soon as I say it, I swear I can see a change in their face as they start to look at me in a different way.

Mr. Henry refills my cup of hot chocolate as I wait for Judd to finish his breakfast. Judd talks nonstop about girls, even with food in his mouth. I have never seen anybody so girl crazy in my entire life. I think, at the present moment he is in love with Lexi, Monika, Chantrelle, Bella, Alicia and a girl he just calls D. He is talking about each one as if she were the only girl in the world for him, and I wonder if they all know about each other.

As we walk the four blocks to the tattoo parlor, Judd talks about Monika again. I give her a fighter's chance in my mind to make it an entire month as his number one. Judd has a brown face like mine and six sisters and no brothers. If I had to bet, most of the girls he mentioned are probably his sisters' friends. He is the middle child. Three of his sisters are older and three are younger. Their mama left town after the last sister was born, and they all live with their daddy. He is not a good man. They live in our building, but thank goodness it is not on the same floor.

The shop is still dark when we get there, and I am surprised when Judd pulls a key out of his pocket.

"When did you get a key?" I ask.

"Last week," he answers, smiling. "I had to make a few promises," he says, smiling again. "No girls."

"I could have guessed that," I say.

Judd walks over to the thermostat and turns up the heat as I look around. Posters fill the walls with illustrations of possible tattoos. Most of them look pretty cheesy to me. Tigers, daggers, barbed wire, suns, moons, snakes, and a bunch of other stuff I would not want on my body forever. I think I would get a plane on my shoulder, just above my bicep. I *am* going to be a pilot.

Judd hands me a stack of flyers, neon blue paper with black writing. I don't read what they say, and Judd doesn't give me direction; I know what I am expected to do.

I walk towards the art college and read faces. I don't waste the papers on old ladies, grumpy looking old guys, frumpy moms, business men, and others who look like they might be opposed to tattoos. I am looking for college kids, edgy adults, artsy types, and people with unique style. I give one to every person with a unique winter hat or scarf. I definitely give one to every person without a coat or even to anyone who is underdressed for the weather. Crazies love tattoos.

The snow falls harder, and I wonder if there will be school tomorrow. Tomorrow is Friday, and if there is no school tomorrow, it will be at least a four day weekend. When my last flyer is handed out, I head back to Hog's. When I arrive I cannot see the sidewalk; I go inside to get the flat-nosed shovel. Mr. Henry smiles but doesn't talk to me as I grab the shovel and head back outside to clean the sidewalk. As I'm shoveling, a plane flies over and I wonder where it is going.

Chapter 3

Back at home, Mama asks me if I have been keeping up with Cecil. She is drinking something that looks like Sprite. This is her favorite drink. I am not allowed to try it. Cecil was supposed to either fix the leak under the kitchen sink or get the super to do it. I tell her I haven't seen him all day, and the answer does not please her.

"When is your brother going to be home?" she says to me; something is obviously wrong with her. She trips across the rug in our kitchen into the living room and I follow her. She stumbles back and forth a couple of times in what I categorize mentally as a shuffle. Upright like a queen she looks at me.

"Your highness," I say.

She laughs and collapses on the couch. She is a crumpled, laughing mess. She shifts her body round and round and the smile deepens with each rotation. When she stops, I wonder if she is dead.

"Mama?" I plead.

"Yeah, baby," she says.

"I love you," I say.

"And I love you," she says. She falls asleep and I kiss her on her forehead as I always do. I cover her with a light blanket.

I walk back into my room and shut the door. The walls of my room are covered with airplanes: posters, magazine pictures, newspaper prints, and drawings. My desk is stacked with papers. One paper in particular catches my eye. It twinkles. Not really—but in my eyes it does. It is a sign advertising an air show. I pulled it off the side of a building last week. I haven't asked Mama if I can go yet. She'll say no anyway.

I know this is hard to believe, but I am eleven years old and I have never been outside of the city. Never. I was born here and sometimes it feels like I'll die here too, without ever leaving. We don't have a car and pretty much walk everywhere; sometimes we take the bus. I hear the door shut and realize either Cecil or grandma is home.

It's grandma. She sees my mama sleeping on the couch and looks at me. "I escape one way and she escapes another," she says. Grandma is holding a stack of books and hands me one. My problems seem to drift away as I see it is a picture book of airplanes.

"Thanks, Grandma." I give her my best smile.

"You're welcome, baby. It was on the shelf with all the brand new books. The librarian said it had never been checked out before. She knows you've seen all the other ones in there."

"I have to show you something, Grandma," I say, running to my room to put the book down and to pick up the advertisement for the air show. I hand it to her and say, "Could you take me to see this?"

"Oh, baby," she says with a frown. "You know if I can't get there by walking I'm not going."

Grandma was in a terrible accident before I was born. She was in a taxi when a bus hit it from the side. The driver of the taxi was killed and she was trapped in the car with his dead body for over an hour while police and firemen worked to pull apart the wrecked metal and get her out. Since a bus was involved in the accident, she thinks buses are just as evil.

"I know," I say. "Maybe Mama will take me."

"Don't you go getting your hopes up. I hate seeing you upset."

Cecil came in the door a few moments later carrying a wrench in each hand.

"Mama here?" he asks, before he was even all the way through the door.

"Sleeping," I answer.

"Did she say anything about the sink?" he asks.

"She was fussing about it when I came in," I answer.

"Super let me borrow these and told me what was probably wrong."

Cecil opens the cabinet doors under the sink, flips over to his back, and slides under the sink like he is fixing a car.

"What did you do today?" Grandma asks Cecil.

"Just went to school," Cecil answers.

"School was cancelled today," Grandma says, rolling her eyes at me.

I laugh as Cecil is probably blushing under the sink. He ignores us. My stomach rumbles and I think of all the good food I ate today. After shoveling the sidewalk at Hog's before lunch, Mr. Henry made me a bacon cheeseburger, fries, and a chocolate milkshake. I can still taste the juicy burger as I look in the freezer and nearly empty refrigerator. The pantry has next to nothing in it as well.

"You cooking or me?" I ask Cecil.

"You."

Grandma doesn't cook. She got burned one time with grease as a little girl and won't even come into the kitchen when the stove is on. Grandma is scared of lots of things. Mama is a pretty good cook when she is awake and we have food. It seems like we usually have lots of food at the beginning of every month and right now we are closer to the end. I guess we run out of money toward the end of every month.

"You want fish sticks, macaroni and cheese with hot dogs cut up in it, or beef stew from a can?"

"What do we have to go with the fish sticks?" Cecil asks, still under the sink.

"We have one can of green beans, a can of pinto beans, or a package of saltine crackers."

"Make the mac and cheese, and fish sticks. Do we have ketchup?"

"Kind of," I answer. "Remember last time you wanted ketchup and it was almost empty, you added a little water and shook it up?"

"OK," Cecil says, climbing out from under the sink.

"Did you fix it?" I ask.

"Yeah. Easy."

"Maybe you could be a plumber," I joke.

Cecil opens the door to go and return the tools. Before he leaves, he says, "Yeah, and maybe you'll be a pilot."

Chapter 4

School is cancelled again on Friday. During the night, another six inches of snow are dumped on the city. Looking out our thirteenth floor window, I don't think I have ever seen our city look so beautiful. I like how it looks at night with all of the lights, but the blanket of white is just beautiful—like something I saw on Charles's television. We have a television, but it doesn't work. It only looks fuzzy when you turn it on. Mama said I could have shoes or cable. I haven't had a new pair of shoes in over a year, so I really don't understand what she is talking about. Shoes must be really expensive. I try not to think bad thoughts about Mama, but I wonder how much her favorite drink costs.

Mr. Henry is glad to see me when I knock on the locked door at five fifteen in the morning. I always get up early, whether there is school or not.

Before he can even wish me a good morning I ask him, "How much is a bus ticket to the city of Chamblee?"

"That's right down the road," he says. "Less than a thirty minute bus ride. Probably cost a couple of bucks each way. Why?"

"An air show is coming in March."

"I saw those papers posted around town. I should have known. Why are you so crazy about planes?"

"I don't know," I answer. "I just love them."

"You just want one of them to take you away from here," Mr. Henry says thoughtfully.

"Maybe," I answer. I walk to the closet where I put the shovel yesterday and grab it. I am getting pretty good at shoveling snow.

When I am finished and walk back into the restaurant, the smell of sausage being cooked attacks my nose and I realize how hungry I am. The macaroni and cheese with fish sticks supper I put together only made enough for one small bowl of noodles and two fish sticks apiece. I went to bed hungry.

"You want the usual?" Mr. Henry asks.

"No," I say.

"What?" Mr. Henry is shocked. This is the first time I have ever said no to an egg sandwich.

"Can I have something with sausage this morning?" I ask.

"You can have the moon, Mash." Mr. Henry gives me a warm smile. "What are your three favorite breakfast foods?" he asks. He already knows the answer, but I guess he wants to hear me say it.

So I say, "Eggs, grits, and this morning, sausage."

We are still the only people in the restaurant. "I am going to make you something I just thought of. It is not even on the menu, but after today, it might have to be."

Mr. Henry hovers over the grill, and without him asking me, I pick up a broom and sweep up a few leaves and things I see under some of the tables. I don't tell him what I am doing, but I see him, out of the corner of my eye, watching me. He smiles like I imagine my dad or granddad might have done if I had one.

"Ready," he calls to me, as the first customer walks in.

I hop up onto one of the stools and see one of his humongous salad bowls sitting on the counter next to a glass of milk. In the bowl are my three favorite things and it looks absolutely delicious. The bowl is filled with grits, chopped up sausage and scrambled eggs all mixed together. Mr. Henry has even topped it all with a light layer of cheese. I look at him and smile and he gives me one of his famous winks.

The customer who has just walked into the door looks into my bowl and asks Mr. Henry what it is.

"That's the Mash Special," he says.

Without thinking, the customer says, "I'll have a cup of coffee and the Mash Special."

I try to cover my laugh, as Mr. Henry grins at me with delight.

That afternoon, Atlanta, Georgia comes back from wherever it has been on vacation. It is fifty degrees by noon and fifty eight degrees by three in the afternoon. I still get another juicy burger for lunch at Hog's because it takes a while for that much snow to melt, and as it melts, it makes a mess of the sidewalk in front of the restaurant.

After I eat the burger, I decide to go visit a friend named Father Phillip. I am not Catholic, but I love Catholics. Some of them go to church every day. They are either very dedicated or they feel guilty about something. Father Phillip is at the church seven days a week. He always, always has good advice. I think part of his job is to give advice.

"Are you here to confess?" he jokes, as I walk into the church.

"Do what?" I ask.

"Confession," he repeats.

"I don't know her," I say. I once knew a girl named Quentishun and what he said reminded me of her.

Father Phillip almost falls down laughing. "I don't know her either," he says, still laughing furiously. When he finally composes himself, he says, "How can I help you, Mash?"

"I need a favor."

"What kind of favor?"

I answer with one word, "Transportation."

Father Phillip looks at me with his kind eyes. "Mash," he says. "I only leave here once a year when I go home to Canada. I don't own a car. I never take the bus. I live my life within five or six city blocks."

"But I have to go."

"If you have to go," Father Phillip says, "then you will. Let me get something for your journey," he says, walking out of the room.

He walks back into the room with something clutched within his hand. He moves his clutched hand

13

toward me and I open my palm to receive whatever it is he has to offer.

He puts a tiny medal in my hand. "This is Saint Christopher," he says. "He is a Saint that watches over travelers. He will keep you safe from harm."

I take the little medal in my hand and put it in my pocket. Father Phillip is looking at me with knowing eyes.

"Do you know something I don't?" I ask.

"I know the same thing you do, Mash. I have counseled thousands of people and I can read eyes. I know that whatever you are talking about is the most important thing in the world to you. I know that no matter what I say—you are going to do it anyway. So why should I waste my breath and try to stop you? I want to keep you safe. Good luck, Mash."

"Thank you for understanding, Father Phillip." I turn and walk out of the church, clutching Saint Christopher in my pocket.

Chapter 5

I actually sleep in Saturday morning until a few minutes before eight. When I get out of bed, Mama is gone. Cecil is still in bed and Grandma is reading.

"Where is Mama?" I ask.

"The check comes today," Grandma answers.

"Oh," I say. The first of the month. Mama gets a check on the first day of every month and she likes to wait for it by the mailbox. Mama gets lots of her favorite drinks on this day and we get lots of new groceries. I smile because tonight we will have a good dinner. We will have good dinners for the next ten days or so. I like the first of the month.

"Are you going to the library today?" I ask Grandma.

"I can," she answers. "Why?"

"Are there bus schedules at the library?"

"I imagine there are," she answers. "If not, the ladies there know how the Internet works and they can find just about anything."

"I want to go with you."

"Let me finish this book and we can go," she says.

As Grandma reads, I go and look again at the air show paper in my room. I memorize the address.

I hear the door shut about an hour later and walk out of my room to find my mama smiling and singing to herself. She has the mail in her hand and is tearing open an envelope. She pulls a piece of paper out of the envelope and sticks it in her front pocket.

"Good morning, Mash," she sings to me.

"Morning, Mama."

"Was I asleep when you came in last night?" she asks.

"Yes ma'am," I answer.

"I had a headache and went to bed early," she says, not looking at me.

"It's OK," I assure her. Since she is in such a good mood I decide it is the perfect time to ask her about taking me to the air show. "Can we go to an air show next month?"

"Somebody is having an air show in the city?" she asks, confused.

"No, it's in Chamblee."

"Oh my," she says. "Let me think about it." Mama walks into her bedroom and calls back to me, "Is it free?"

"It's twenty five dollars a person," I say, knowing this will be the end of the conversation.

"Twenty five dollars a person!" she screams. If the two of us go, it will be fifty bucks!" Mama storms out of her room toward me and I hold up my hands in surrender.

"OK. OK. Forget it. I just thought I would ask. I didn't mean to upset you."

Mama puts some ice in a cup and pours herself a little drink. She takes a big swallow and plops down at the kitchen table. Her shoulders relax and so does her face.

"I'm sorry Mash. For our family, fifty dollars is a whole lot of money. If I had an extra fifty dollars, I would take you for sure." She finishes her drink and says, "I'm sorry," again.

"I said it's OK," I say, giving her a hug.

At the library, Grandma disappears to find more books. After looking around unsuccessfully for bus information, I go to the counter and wait for the librarian to finish checking in a stack of books.

I ask her for a bus schedule to Chamblee and she tells me I will have to take the MARTA train first and then transfer to a bus. She digs around under the counter and pulls out a few different folders, looks at different pamphlets, and finally hands me three different ones.

"I think you will find everything you need in these," she says.

"Thank you so much," I answer.

I sit down at a table and try to figure out a route. I search the charts and maps for a few minutes before I decide I will need help. I decide to go to the tattoo shop later to ask Judd for his help. He travels all over the city and he will know how to read the maps and schedules.

When I walk into Art Inkorporated, Gina tells me that Judd is with a customer. Judd hears my voice and yells for me to come on back to his studio area. A giant man who looks like a Santa Claus gone wrong is sitting in his chair. Judd is hovered over him with his tattooing pen in one hand and a paper towel in the other wiping away blood. I make a mental note to never get a tattoo as it looks incredibly painful. The bad Santa does not seem to mind.

His tattoo has a woman, who I doubt is his wife or girlfriend, and fire. Judd has started something else that looks evil. On his other arm is a snake decorated with a stream of numbers that don't seem to make any sense whatsoever. Bad Santa asks Judd if he can take a break and go outside to smoke a cigarette, and Judd agrees that he needs a break.

"What's up little man?" Judd asks.

"How much would it cost for me to get that same tattoo?" I ask, not cracking a smile.

Judd doesn't know what to say at first. Finally he says, "Your mama would kill *me* and *you*."

I smile. "I'm kidding. I need help reading these MARTA maps and schedules."

"I don't need those," Judd says. "I know how to get everywhere. Where are you going?"

"Peachtree Dekalb Airport. Most people call it PDK."

"Give me the maps and schedules. Never heard of that one."

I hand Judd the information and he studies it thoughtfully. Evil Santa comes back into the room

17

smelling of cigarette smoke and tells Judd he is ready to continue.

"Come back later today or tomorrow and I'll tell you what I figured out," Judd says to me.

"OK," I say.

Little did I know I would see bad Santa again.

Part II

Chapter 6

Juniper and his sister Junior sat in Juniper's spacious art studio. Juniper sat in a leather rocking lounger with his feet up, as Junior filed his toenails. She did anything he said—she had the brains of a field mouse, with the mental edge going to the field mouse. Juniper gazed to the ceiling where he had painted a picture of himself floating in a perfect blue sky, staring back at anyone who might look into his eyes. Juniper stared into his own eyes and smiled. He loved himself.

The art studio actually was a gigantic red barn. That is the way it looked on the outside anyways. The inside was a state-of-the-art studio that would have Pablo Picasso and all the world's most famous artists wagging their tongues with jealousy. It had kilns and wheels for ceramics. It had welding equipment, blocks of marble, stacks of metal. It had easels by the dozen, tubes of paint by the hundreds, brushes and palettes and odds and ends like one has never seen. Money was obviously not an object when it came to what Juniper Jenkins wanted. He had it all.

His mother and father were dead and gone, but their money was still alive and well. Mother Jenkins, in her life, was a devoted protector of the environment. She rallied for dolphins, protested against bulldozers, and held vigils for people she didn't even know. You might classify her as a hippy. She hugged a tree or two in her day.

Father Jenkins golfed at one o'clock every afternoon. Drink black coffee, read the paper, worry, and golf. That was his daily routine. Oh... because of *his* parents, he was stinking, filthy rich. He worried the money would go away and golf took his mind off the money. He was never around when Juniper and Junior came home from school, as he chose a little place called the Nineteenth Hole over home after the golfing.

With the whacked out ideals from his mother and the anger over his father's absence, Juniper somehow let all of those feelings and ideas turn him into a sometimes angry but mostly playful artist. I guess one could say that Juniper liked to mess with people. He liked people to see his art and feel confusion, hilarity, disbelief, or horror, just to name a few of the emotions he wished to evoke.

Junior, who once upon a time was called Willow (don't forget the hippy mom), never advanced past a six or seven year old mind. She didn't want any part of the crazy upbringing, so she mentally checked out and never fully checked back in. She protected herself in the only way she knew, by blocking it all out.

On the day the blockage began, Mr. Jenkins came home early from the Nineteenth Hole. He had made a hole-in-one that day. He had obviously been celebrating. He ran over the mailbox and trenched the front yard as he parked his car on top of the swing set. Willow had been playing in a sandbox nearby. The car skidded through the front yard, barreled around the side of the house, and finally slid, flipped exactly once, and landed right side up crushing the swing set flat. Pieces of metal and the cheap plastic seats landed in the sandbox, followed by the car keys. Mr. Jenkins stumbled out of the car, tossed his keys to Willow and said, "Park it in my normal spot, Junior." Somehow the name stuck.

"I'm getting bored again, Junior," Juniper said as she finished up on his toes.

"Uh oh," was all she said.

"Don't say uh oh. I am changing the world with my art. People are thinking about art because of me. Art is *not* dead. It may be on life support, but I won't let it die. Mother would be happy."

"Mom would have liked the duckies."

"Yeah," Juniper smiled, thinking of the rubber duckies.

A year earlier, Juniper had purchased ten thousand rubber duckies. At noon, on one of the busiest tourist days of the year at Niagara Falls, he dumped them upstream. As people stood marveling at the beauty of the falls, their amazement shot to a different level entirely as the yellow rubber ducks began to slide over the falls. They kept coming and coming and at one point the entire wall of the falls appeared to be yellow. Juniper had the pictures to prove it. He glanced at the massive photo of the event hanging in the studio and thought about how cool and clever he was.

"It was on the news for weeks," Juniper said proudly.

"Never caught us," Junior added.

"Nope. We're too good."

"Almost got caught in Washington, D.C.," Junior put forth.

"Yeah," Juniper said. "That security there was almost too much."

In the National Mall, a National Park in the nation's capital, stands the Lincoln Memorial to honor the country's sixteenth president, Abraham Lincoln. The building itself is modeled after a Greek Doric temple. Inside the temple, sits a mammoth marble sculpture of a seated Abraham Lincoln. The Georgia white marble sculpture is nineteen feet tall and sits on a ten foot pedestal.

On the day of the Washington, D.C. "art installment," Juniper employed the help of an old pal who looked exactly like Santa Claus. In the middle of July, dressed in the red suit, with a huge red bag flung over his shoulder, he started ho ho hoing and reaching into his bag grabbing and handing out wrapped presents. People flocked around him and security's attention was diverted long enough for Juniper to add something to the massive Abraham Lincoln statue.

As people tore the gift wrap off the presents and discovered ipods inside, everyone rushed out of the memorial to get a gift from Santa. Alone inside, Juniper took at least ten wonderful pictures of old Abe in his new digs.

When Santa disappeared just as fast as he had appeared and the security guards gained their wits again, they discovered that someone in all of the confusion and excitement, had placed a giant, custom made ball cap on Mr. Lincoln's head. The hat read "NRA" and had a black silhouette of a handgun.

Juniper turned his gaze to the photo of which he had mailed a copy to every news organization he knew. Inside the anonymous letters, he stamped a picture of a rubber ducky as his signature and the media had made the connection.

"I don't want to get hot again," Junior said.

"I know you didn't like that one," Juniper answered.

Junior was referring to the time they had taken their artistic talents to Death Valley in Eastern California. Death Valley is the driest, hottest, and lowest point in North America. It is within the Mojave Desert and gets an average of two inches of rain per year. It is very rare to see flowers. When flowers are actually seen in the desert, people call it the hundred year bloom. Seeds will sit dormant on the desert floor for decades until enough rain comes along to give them the conditions necessary to make flowers. It happened in 2005. No one thought it would happen again in their lifetime.

Juniper, with help of the man who played Santa and handed out gifts at the Lincoln Memorial, assembled a crew of hard working men and women who would keep their mouths shut. The generous amount of money they were paid was not only for their hard work, but also for their silence. Immediately after dark, during the hottest part of the year, his crews began to work and worked furiously all night until a hint of the morning sun appeared in the Eastern sky. Like a crew of vampires, they fled from the light.

What the men and women left behind was one of the most beautiful things Juniper could ever remember seeing. After taking a shower at a seedy motel and having

23

a cup of coffee, he hopped onto a rented BMW motorcycle and drove toward Badwater, a basin within Death Valley. His camera sat ready in one of the saddle bags. Sand and desolation lay as far as the eye could see. As Juniper pulled back on the motorcycle's throttle, he felt as though he was travelling through an alien landscape.

Rounding a bend, he saw the previous night's work and he braked hard as his breath left his body. The sight was more beautiful than he even imagined it would be. Thousands upon thousands of artificial roses were planted in the sand. Red, white, and yes, blue. Their beauty and color contrasting against the bleak sand was mesmerizing. The enormity of the task hit Juniper and a tear rolled down his cheek. He had taken six months to plan this one and it had surpassed his lofty expectations. He pulled out his Nikon and began snapping pictures.

Juniper thought of the Death Valley bloom as his masterpiece. The photo hung over his desk in the studio. He studied it, as Junior studied him. Juniper tried to think of what he could do next.

"Buy me ice-cream," Junior said.

Juniper's eyes flashed with an idea. "You're a genius," he screamed. "Ice-cream it is!"

Chapter 7

Juniper bought Junior a triple scoop of ice cream with three different flavors smushed into a waffle cone. Juniper thought it looked nasty. The flavor on top was called peach cobbler crunch, and it had real peach pieces sticking out, ruining the perfect sphere that Juniper thought should top a cone. Under the peach scoop sat the second flavor, marshmallow madness. Juniper thought he might throw up when he saw the marshmallows popping out of the frozen ice cream with peach juice running down and mingling with the fluffy white. At the bottom of Junior's strange creation, holding it all together—a house specialty, only available here or in Brazil where it is wildly popular, corn. Yes, you read that correctly—corn. Not only corn flavored, but containing real pieces of corn as well.

Mr. Teca, a Brazilian man, owned the ice cream shop and had tried for years to win over the locals with the corn flavor which in his home country sold more than all of the other flavors. Only Junior and a very few others had joined the craze here in the States and he beamed every time he saw her. He called her Miss Rio after his home city, Rio de Janeiro.

"That is the most delicious cone I see today," Mr. Teca announced.

"It would be even better if you had a lima bean ice cream flavor," Junior commented.

"Lima bean!" Mr. Teca hollered. "Lima bean!" He turned around in circles three times screaming the words. "You are a genius, Miss Rio." Juniper tried to hand Mr. Teca a five dollar bill to pay for the ice cream and he shoved Juniper's hand out of his way and said, "For your sister, free of charge. She gives great idea. Lima bean, lima bean, lima bean." Mr. Teca kept chanting his lima bean mantra back into the store room and away from Juniper and Junior.

Junior acted as though nothing had happened, as Juniper stuck the five dollar bill into the tip jar on the serving counter. He looked around to see if he was being punked on some crazy reality television show or if aliens were here to take him to their home planet to perform an array of invasive tests on his human body. Nope, he finally decided. Junior and Mr. Teca just had underdeveloped taste buds, he thought. *Lima beans and corn in ice cream?*

Juniper studied Junior as they sat at one of the picnic tables the ice cream parlor provided. She was deep into her licking and didn't notice him staring. Even if she did, she would not have cared. Juniper noticed how pretty her brown hair appeared in the sunlight. A ray of light highlighted her cheekbone and Juniper took a snapshot in his mind; his ditzy sister was quite pretty. Dumb as rocks, but cute as a kitten. He smiled, knowing he would probably have to look out for her for the rest of their lives and this made him happy. Junior made the perfect companion for him. Quiet when his brain needed to explore deep thoughts, agreeable when he needed a sounding board, and willing when he needed a partner in one of his crazy schemes.

Juniper turned his gaze away from his sister and studied the ice cream parlor, wondering if there would be a poster or sign anywhere announcing the brand of ice cream that was served. Juniper found his answer written in a tiny script below the menu of flavors—King Cone. He grinned a wide and mischievous Cheshire Cat grin.

Back at the new home office, the executives of King Cone sat around an enormous table. The giant table's length stretched as long as most peoples' driveways. Men and women in expensive suits gathered around the table to discuss the ribbon cutting of their new building. The new King Cone building, located in downtown Atlanta, Georgia stretched high above every other building in the city. Until now, the Bank of America building held the title of the tallest building in the Atlanta cityscape *and* the ninth tallest building in the United States. Say hello to

26

number ten, Bank of America. King Cone execs on the top floor can now look down on you and your fifty-five stories and your one thousand and twenty three foot tall building.

The King Cone building also had fifty-five regular stories. Beyond that, stood a new marvel for the Atlanta skyline. Above, stood an enormous replication of a soft serve ice cream cone holding inside six additional stories of office space for the executives. The architects had spent countless hours making sure this element of the building wowed not only Atlanta but the entire world. The enormity of the cone could be seen clearly from the highways, travelling in and out of the city, as well as from airplanes taking off from and landing at Hartsfield Jackson International Airport. The pure white of the ice cream swirl sitting atop the *real* gold plated cone, which was fashioned after the gold plating on the Georgia capital building, mesmerized everyone that laid eyes on it.

Stuart King, sitting at the head of the table, called the meeting to order saying, "Listen up y'all." The room immediately went silent. Although Stuart King was a southern gentleman, he was also a shrewd businessman and everyone who knew what was right and what was wrong was scared to pieces of Mr. King. He had an easy smile and a gentle demure way about him. His genteel nature could lead one down the wrong road to thinking he could easily be pushed to the side and passed by. He could not.

"I am afraid our grand opening ceremonies planned for today will have to be cancelled." He paused to take the pulse of the room. When nobody moved or said a word, he continued. "I am moving the grand opening of the building to March," he announced. "We can tie it in with spring and rebirth and the comeback of everybody's favorite treat—ice cream." He paused again, waiting for a discussion from the group. When one did not begin, he announced, "You are all free to go home."

Stuart, although he was the head of King Cone, had fallen out of love with the ice cream business. He *had*

27

fallen in love with music. The inside of the cone had a secret "attic" and Stuart was the only one in the entire world who knew of its existence, besides the architects, of course. They were sworn to some sort of death pact. Of the six stories inside of the cone, the top held Stuart's office. Inside a locked closet in the office stood a lift which, when a special key was inserted into its lock, would rise as the ceiling simultaneously opened up to accept its entry.

The secret attic not only had Stuart's office space in between it and the other offices to conceal the sounds he made, but the architects used twice the recommended amounts of noise dampening materials to hide sound per Stuart's request. To test the effectiveness of the distance and the materials, Stuart cranked the sound system up with Eminem's latest album and strolled through the floor just below his office, as others were quietly working at their desks. Nobody noticed a thing and Stuart tried and tried to hear something, but he could not.

After Stuart told everybody to go home for the day, he watched as they all walked back to their offices grinning. He walked over to his personal secretary's desk and asked, "Ken, why isn't everybody going home?"

Sheepishly, Ken answered, saying, "We all actually have a lot of work to do, Mr. King. When we switched offices, we lost a lot of time and most of us are really, really behind in our work."

"How many times do I have to tell you to call me, Stuart?"

"Mr. King," Ken began, "I know I'm new, but may I please speak freely for a moment?"

"You can speak freely all the time. I didn't hire you to kiss my feet!"

"Mr. King, you are probably worth a hundred million dollars at least. I am an administrative assistant."

"Is this your way of asking me for a raise, Kevin?"

"It's Ken. And no, I am not asking for a raise. I have only been here a couple of weeks."

"Don't you want to make more money, Kenny?"

"Well, of course I do."

"Call me Stuart and I'll double your pay."

Ken's eye's grew three sizes like the Grinch's heart as he said, "OK Mr. Stuart."

"Nope," Stuart said.

"Stuart, sir?" Ken tried.

"Nope."

"OK, Stuart," Ken finally spit out.

"Great!" Stuart said. "You got yourself a raise."

"Thank you... Stuart," Ken said.

"OK. Hold my calls for two hours, Keith. I have a few things to do."

"It's Ken, Mr., I mean Stuart, sir, I mean Stuart."

Stuart did not hear him, as he thought of his music studio. He usually remembered every name after meeting a person only one time. After being bitten by the music bug, he had started to become distracted with his thoughts slipping away to his guitars and riffs and lyrics and recording all of the musical happenings that had taken over in his head.

Stuart locked the door to his office and checked it twice. He then unlocked the closet which held the lift, walked inside, and locked it behind him. He inserted the key into the lift and it began to rise. As it rose, the ceiling above him parted and the lights in the studio automatically turned on. He felt as if he were ascending into heaven.

As the lift came to a stop, he looked around the room. On guitar stands scattered throughout the room, he had at least a dozen guitars of the best quality available: electric, six string acoustic, twelve string acoustic, bass guitars, even two mandolins and a banjo. Stuart had a super-computer built just for recording music and he had a specially built microphone that cost eleven thousand dollars. An eleven thousand dollar microphone! He had harmonicas in all the keys available, a drum kit, a saxophone he barely knew how to play and piles and piles of notes and songs he had written or was in the process of writing.

Stuart sat down in a chair without an armrest on the right side, so he could sit back and hold his guitar unimpeded. He tuned the guitar with the help of an auto tuner hooked up to his computer, and once tuned, he sunk into the chair and closed his eyes to strum.

Chapter 8

Back at home, Junior went to the house and Juniper headed back to his studio. Phineas and Ferb, a cartoon show, came on at four and Junior did not like to miss her Phineas and Ferb. Juniper liked it as well, but he had seen all of the new episodes and needed a little alone time to think about his new scheme.

In the studio, Juniper had a laptop computer which talked to a wireless router in the main house to get the Internet. Technology! It amazed Juniper. He also had a small television set to watch baseball games when he was working in the studio. There was just something about the pace of the game and the announcers that put him in the mood to work. He had a satellite dish installed and it never ceased to astonish him that it all worked. Somewhere, hovering above the earth was a satellite beaming down baseball games to him! Astonishing!

He hopped onto the information highway and Googled pictures of the subject of his new project. Juniper found one with a large resolution and saved it to his desktop. He sat back and stared at it. *Perfect*, he thought. *Perfect. All I need now is a plane and supplies*, he thought.

Juniper's thoughts turned to a color. He had an array of oil and acrylic paints at his disposal as well as a few hundred pre-mixed colors. This job, he thought, needed a custom color of his making. Juniper went to work squirting a dab of this and a dab of that on a piece of glass he used as a palette, and he mixed as he went with a plastic knife from Wendy's, knowing in his mind just what he was looking for. He worked like a mad scientist, focused and driven to find the color he saw in his mind. Finally, after twelve or so other pigments and a teeny squeeze of yellow ochre, he had it. He stood back, studied it from a few different angles and finally screamed, "Voila!"

Juniper flipped through the Rolodex in his mind and stopped when it landed on the guy he knew could get him a large quantity of paint mixed to this exact color. He pictured the man clearly in his mind and said aloud, "Ho, ho, ho!"

Juniper pulled up the sleeve on his left arm revealing a pass code tattooed in his skin, which circled and twisted around a design in a way only he knew how to read. He, in a fit of paranoia, had devised an elaborate scheme to know he was talking to one of his people over the telephone. Five people had the tattoos, each with different pass codes. Four of the people he employed in his schemes had never seen him and only knew his voice from the phone. The jobs he paid them for were mostly setup work or diversions. Juniper had paid them handsomely to get the tattoos and only he knew exactly how the system worked.

Juniper opened a drawer and pulled out a prepaid cell phone that could not be traced back to him and dialed another phone just like it. The voice on the other end of the line answered as instructed, saying, "I'm ready," which meant to Juniper that he could talk. If the voice answered "Hello," Juniper would hang up as that meant it was not safe to talk. Then he would try back exactly twenty minutes later, giving the voice on the other end time to wrap up whatever he was doing without suspicion and get to a safe place to talk.

Juniper said, "2, 7, 9, 1, 4, square, triangle, 9, 2, rectangle, 1, 1, 7."

The voice on the other end answered, "4, 14, 18, 2, 8, 4, 3, 18, 4, 4, 2, 2, 14."

"You may speak freely," Juniper said. A tricky grin crept across his face. He loved the cloak-and-dagger tactics almost as much as he loved the art.

"What can I do for you, boss?"

"I am going to do a job in Atlanta and I am going to need a lot of paint," Juniper answered.

The voice on the other end of the line knew not to ask what the job was. He had learned from experience that he would know when the time was right if he needed to know. Sometimes he only knew when he watched the news. Whatever the reason, he had learned to trust that Juniper would not put him in any danger of getting in trouble with the law.

"I am assuming," the voice said, "that this is going to be a special paint? Either a special color or am I sensing you also may need a special way of applying this paint?"

This was one of the things Juniper loved about the man on the other end of the line whom he called Nick. Nick never asked what he was doing and Juniper never had to tell him not to ask. Also, even though Nick did not know what he was up to, he had a strange sixth sense which seemed to guide him toward what Juniper needed.

"Both," Juniper answered. "Let's focus on the color first. I have mixed up a color that I would like you to match exactly. By my very quick and crude calculations, I think I might want a hundred gallons of this color in something that will be used on an exterior surface. It needs to stick on contact if possible. It will need to be poured or be delivered in a very quick manner. I'll let that be your problem."

"Yes sir," Nick said, nodding his head to himself.

Nick wondered, but he would never ask about the pay, knowing his boss paid him generously for every job.

"This is going to be my masterpiece," Juniper said, staring at the photo of Death Valley, which he considered up to now to be his masterpiece. "Do you remember what I paid you for the Death Valley job?"

"Yes sir, I do."

"I am paying five times that much for you on this job."

"Thank you, sir," Nick answered with a jolt of surprise in his voice.

"Let me tell you why," Juniper said.

"OK."

"Well," Juniper began. "I know all about you and your connections and have no doubt you will get me the perfect paint I need, exactly matched to the sample I am going to put in the mail to you tomorrow. I also found out something else about you recently that has increased your worth to me."

"What is that, sir?" Nick asked.

"I learned you have another hobby besides motorcycles."

"Yes sir, I do."

"So, although I am pretty sure I know, tell me what your other hobby is."

"I fly planes, sir. I am a pilot."

Part III

Chapter 9

By Sunday afternoon, all traces of the snow have disappeared. I can hardly believe the snow ever happened. I shut myself in my room to do the homework I have been putting off because of the weather. Mama never asks if I have done my homework or if I even have any. Grandma doesn't either. My teacher, Ms. Monique knows that Mama is too distracted to worry about my school life and she told me it is *my* responsibility to get my work finished. She teaches me all kinds of things besides my school subjects. I used to always be late for school because I stayed up late and slept in. Mama sleeps until ten almost every morning; her special drink makes her really sleepy. So, Ms. Monique bought me an alarm clock and taught me how to set it so it will wake me up. She told me it would be a good habit to get in bed by eight thirty on school nights and read for a half hour or so before turning out the light. I do it every school night. I even turn on a small fan to block out the noise in our building.

Mama is yelling at someone on the phone and stumbling around when I come out of my room. Grandma is sitting in her chair reading a book as if she were sitting alone on a tranquil deserted island. I don't know how she blocks it all out. Mama is saying something about how she didn't sign her name to any checks. She went away one time for writing bad checks. Two years. Grandma did alright while Mama was in jail. Life was probably even better, really. Mama seems to attract problems.

I kiss Grandma goodnight and wave goodnight to Mama who doesn't see me. Cecil is supposedly at work. He is such a liar. I don't consider working sitting on a corner step and trading money for evils. He always has money he keeps for himself and I don't want it anyway; dirty money is no good. I think Cecil has taken the path of laziness.

The next morning at school, the day begins with all the kids trading snow stories. Charles sits next to me and asks why I wasn't out playing in the snow like all the other kids. He has a shiner around his right eye where he proudly told me he was hit by a snowball that must have been pure ice.

"Is your phone turned off again?" Charles asks.

"Yep," I answer. "Seems to stay that way, doesn't it."

"Yeah," he says thoughtfully. "I would have come and got you, but I knew if you could be out there you would have been. Were you working at Hog's for Mr. Henry?"

"Yep. That and doing a little work for Judd. I'm saving up for something."

"What?"

"Have you seen those air show posters all over town?"

"Yeah."

"I'm going. Tickets are twenty-five dollars each and I might have to take the train and a bus or two."

"Oh man," Charles says. "I have never been that far! Is that in Georgia?"

"Yes. I don't think MARTA goes out of Georgia."

As soon as I say that, Ms. Monique enters the room and the students stop all of their conversations and sit down. They do not do this for all the teachers, but they all respect and love Ms. Monique. She smiles, knowing she has all of our attention.

Ms. Monique speaks with an accent. Sometimes I wonder if it is why all the kids are so mesmerized by her. My school is a pretty rough place and I have seen the kids run off more than a few adults who thought they were up to the task of teaching in the city. I liken her in my mind to a snake charmer. Her voice leads the class like a snake charmer's instrument with a hypnotic sound that puts the venomous ones among us at ease. She somehow manages a class without *ever* raising her voice.

She is a tiny lady with what most people call white skin. I don't know why people call skin color white and black. I'm not really black and she really isn't white. Her hair is short, and sometimes when she comes to school, it is still wet. I have a feeling she is not a morning person, and that is why she likes to start every day with a writing project. After we start writing, she makes a cup of tea and slowly walks around the room waking up. I think she might not have a lot of money like I thought teachers did because she usually uses the same tea bag at least three times.

I think the thing I like about Ms. Monique the most is that she asks me a lot of questions. Mama almost never asks me questions unless the answer has to do with her well being. With her questions, Ms. Monique makes me think about things I would have never thought about on my own. The second best thing about her is her laugh. She loves to laugh.

"I think we should spend some time this morning writing about our experiences with the snow," Ms. Monique begins. "Your writing can be a true story, or you may use your imagination and add any other elements you would like, such as werewolves or airplanes," she says, looking at me. I always have airplanes in my stories.

As the students get out their paper and sharpen pencils, Ms. Monique fills her mug with water and walks into her supply closet where she keeps a microwave. I hear the click of the door opening and the bleep, bleep, bleep, of her pushing buttons, followed by the whirl of the microwave doing its thing warming up her water. If most teachers were in a walk-in closet with their eyes away from the students, mayhem would occur. When Ms. Monique walks out of the closet, all the students are settled at their desks working or thinking. She walks to her desk and drops a new tea bag into the cup and takes a stroll around the room doing what she calls her celebrations—she is pumping us up by giving us compliments.

Chapter 10

That afternoon, walking home from school, I can't believe my eyes, as I look into the front window of Hog's. The evil Santa character is sitting at the counter eating a burger. I had intended to go straight home to do my homework, but I decide to stop in to get another look at him. Something about the tattoo with all the numbers is under my skin and I don't know why.

Mr. Henry sees me, as I walk in the door. As usual, he is hovering over the grill which can be seen from just about anywhere in the restaurant. He waves a hand at me telling me to come into the kitchen area. I walk through the restaurant and push through the swinging double doors leading to the back, without glancing at evil Santa. I don't know if he will recognize me from the tattoo parlor, but I don't want to take a chance. He might think I am following him, which in a way I am.

"Hey Mash," Mr. Henry says, genuinely happy to see me. "How was school today?"

I walk to a spot which cannot be seen from the restaurant's sitting area before I answer him. "It was school."

"I'm afraid I don't have any work for you today," he says, "but how about a milkshake on the house?" Mr. Henry gives me a smile.

"Oh," I say. "Umm... not today, but thanks."

Mr. Henry flips whatever it is he is cooking and gives me a weird look. "What's going on?" he asks. "Why are you standing over there with that weird look on your face?"

Without saying anything I point my finger toward the dining room. Mr. Henry looks into the dining room where evil Santa sits at the counter, and an older lady is waiting for her food in a booth, patiently reading a book. The rest of the seats are empty, as three thirty in the afternoon is not a peak time for meals.

"I am guessing you are not hiding from anyone," he whispers. I shake my head from side to side. "The gentleman at the counter?" I shake my head up and down. "What did he do to you? Or what did you do to him?" he asks.

He walks over to where I am standing so I can whisper to him. "I saw him at Judd's tattoo parlor."

"He does have a lot of those."

"Something about him isn't right," I say, my voice full of conspiracy.

"What?" Mr. Henry asks.

"Don't you think he looks a little bit like somebody?" I say. "I mean, come on!"

"OK," Mr. Henry admits. "He looks like Santa."

"Santa does *not* have tattoos."

"He is not the real Santa."

I look at Mr. Henry like he has seven heads and a tail. "I know he is not the real Santa, but don't you think the Santa look and tattoos just don't mix?"

"I hate to say this Mash, but white people all look the same to me. Santa or no Santa. To me, he is an old white guy with tattoos."

"I need you to do me a favor," I ask.

"If it will get you off this subject I will do anything," Mr. Henry says.

"Ask him the meaning of the tattoo with all the numbers."

"OK," Mr. Henry concedes. "I did think that one was kind of weird."

Mr. Henry finishes cooking over the grill and delivers the meal to Mrs. Modine. He makes small talk with her for about a minute and moseys back to the counter to check up on evil Santa. I watch as he fills his coffee and once again makes small talk, but I cannot hear what he is saying. Evil Santa smiles and shakes his head up and down and points to the opposite arm of the tattoo in which I am interested. Mr. Henry pulls up his sleeve and points to a tattoo I didn't know existed. Evil Santa

42

laughs and laughs and laughs. I can't wait to ask Mr. Henry about his tattoo. Mr. Henry points to evil Santa's other arm and evil Santa's face goes blank. He says something briskly to Mr. Henry and turns his face down to his plate. Mr. Henry turns and walks away.

With wild eyes, Mr. Henry walks back into the kitchen. He motions with his head for me to follow him and he opens the door to the walk-in freezer. We walk in and he shuts the door.

Still with wide eyes, he says, "I think you are right, Mash. There is something very mysterious about that tattoo. Before I asked him about it, he was so friendly and talkative. After I asked him about it, he completely shut down and shut me out. What do you think it is?"

"I have no idea," I answer. "Why don't you lift up your sleeve and show me yours, though," I say with a smile on my face.

Mr. Henry looks at me as if he would like to throw *me* onto the grill and smiles as he lifts his sleeve. Bugs Bunny is boxing Daffy Duck on his left shoulder and I don't know what to say.

"It is actually a long story," Mr. Henry says.

"I bet it is," I answer. "I have to go home and do my homework."

As I start to walk out of the kitchen, Mr. Henry stops me and asks, "Mash, please don't tell anybody about the tattoo, please."

"Your secret is safe with me," I say as I chuckle a little. Mr. Henry hears me giggle and laughs himself.

As I am leaving, I hear him say to no one and every one, "Oh, the foolish things we humans do!"

A few minutes after I leave Hog's, I walk into Art Inkorporated. I still need to be at home doing my homework, but something about the tattoo with all of the numbers has me uneasy. Gina, who is on the phone, is working the desk and points her thumb toward the back. I don't know if she is telling me Judd is in the back or to go on back, so I interpret her gesture to mean that I should go on back and find Judd. When I walk past the lobby area, she doesn't say a word and I feel as if I have made the right choice. I hear the buzz of the tattoo needle as I near Judd's area and I wonder what kind of freak I will encounter when I get there.

Judd has the curtain to his area drawn and I knock on the wooded area around the curtain to be polite. He says to come in, and when I do, I am shocked to see who is in the chair. It is Father Phillip.

I can tell by the look in his eyes that he is a bit surprised to see me as well. He recovers well and smiles his gentle smile.

"I didn't expect to see you here," Father Phillip says.

"You are just about the last person I would have thought would be sitting in Judd's chair getting a tattoo," I answer.

Father Phillip and Judd burst out laughing and I think for a moment that Father Phillip is going to fall out of the chair and roll around on the ground with his outburst.

"I am not getting a tattoo," Father Phillip says.

I look to Judd. "I heard your tattoo needle buzzing as I came down the hall," I protest.

"I was just showing him how it works," Judd answers. He is smiling ear to ear as he thinks the situation and my obvious reaction is incredibly comical. "I don't think priests get tattoos, do they?" he asks, turning to Father Phillip.

"I don't know any who have one, but I don't think there is anything wrong with it. The Bible does say that the body is a temple, but I don't see why God would have a problem with some people decorating their temple."

"I hope God's cool like that," Judd says. "What do you need, Mash?" He asks me, changing the subject.

"I didn't mean to interrupt your conversation with Father Phillip," I answer. "Why don't I come back later?" I offer.

"We have just finished our conversation," Father Phillip says, getting up from the tattooing chair. "Thank you for your advice," he says, patting Judd on the shoulder. Judd reaches out his hand and they vigorously pump each others' fist. "Good to see you, Mash," he says to me, rubbing my head.

After Father Phillip walks through the curtained doorway, I wait a few moments until I feel sure he is out of the building. Judd is just watching me and waiting for what I have to say. He has a little grin on his face that I don't like too much.

"I didn't know you knew Father Phillip," I begin.

"Do you know everybody I know?" Judd asks. He still has a slight turn of a grin at the corners of his mouth, and for some reason this makes me angry.

"I have a very good feeling that you are not Catholic," I begin. "And forgive me for being suspicious, but I can't even begin to imagine where you might have been to meet Father Phillip. He does not go to clubs where you go, he does not hang out in tattoo parlors, and he doesn't chase women like you do—so no, I don't know everybody you do, but I have a very good—no, *great* feeling that you don't know Father Phillip." I take a breath and continue. "My teacher today already gave me a little lecture about wanting to go to the air show and I come here to ask you a simple question and find you speaking with a friend of mine and it makes me think you two are somehow trying to get me from not going, too." I take another breath and wait for Judd's response.

"Mash! Mash! Mash! Mash!" Judd says, shaking his head from side to side. "I don't like to get all touchy feely little bro, but listen up. I do kind of think of you as a little brother and I care for you. I don't want to see you get yourself into any kind of big time trouble. You *are* only eleven."

"I know how old I am," I say, softening a bit.

Judd continues. "Eleven year olds don't go on trips across town to whole new other cities to do *anything*. You are eleven! I know you are wise beyond your years and you have had to grow up fast because of your mama, but you are still eleven."

"I know," I say.

"I heard you telling Mr. Henry one time that Father Phillip was a friend whom you could trust with your secrets."

"I guess I can't trust him anymore."

"He didn't tell me anything I didn't already know!" Judd almost yells. "You asked me how to get there. I just wanted his advice on whether I should help you out by telling you how to get there or not. He didn't tell me anything I didn't already know," Judd says again, trying to protect Father Phillip. "Priests are not allowed to tell anybody what you tell them. You can tell one that you killed a guy and he won't tell anybody."

I look at the floor, feeling better that Father Phillip did not betray me but sad that Judd will probably not help me. I start to wonder how I will find out how to get to the airport where the air show is being held. I am sure with a little thinking and some more research that I will be able to figure it out.

Snapping back to the moment at hand I ask Judd, "So, what is Father Phillip's advice?"

Without speaking, Judd goes over to his drafting table and picks up a piece of paper. He pretends he is reading it, just to make me wait a moment longer.

With a smile, Judd turns to me and says, "He told me to tell you how to get there."

I can hardly believe my good luck as I walk home with a skip in my step. I am surprised Father Phillip told Judd it was OK to give me directions. I am more surprised when I enter my apartment and Cecil is standing at the stove making dinner.

"Do I smell chili?" I ask. I smell something else that smells a little strange but it quickly leaves my mind.

"Yep," he says. "I forgot we had those hot dogs in the back of the fridge. I saw those this morning and stopped by the store on my way home and picked up some buns and a can of chili."

"You feeling, OK?" I ask.

"Be quiet and fix yourself a couple of dogs on me!"

Cecil hands me a plate and we chow down.

Chapter 11

At three o'clock the next morning I awake and sit straight up in bed. My stomach feels like it is on fire. I feel things that are not normal happening inside my body and my throat starts to quiver. Sweat droplets begin to form on my forehead and the room spins a little bit. I think back to the supper Cecil cooked and remember the hot dogs smelling odd. I burp a pre-throw up burp and taste hot dog and know for sure that the hot dogs are responsible for what I am feeling. My tummy rumbles again and I know that throwing up is going to happen whether I want it or not. I hate throwing up.

I get up and open the door to my bedroom and wait for my eyes to adjust to the darkness of the living room. Once they have adjusted, I see a lump on the couch and hear deep snoring. Mama is asleep with all of her clothes on and even her shoes.

My stomach heaves and I rush to the bathroom quickly, turning on the light and shutting the door. As soon as I get over the toilet, it begins. My eyes water as my stomach empties itself of the hot dogs and more. I heave and I heave until nothing else comes and I feel my body relax as it has thrown out the unwanted intruders. I flush the toilet and sit a moment gathering my strength and catching my breath.

Once my breathing returns to normal, I pull myself up and stare at my face in the mirror. I look horrible. I splash water in my face a few times and brush my teeth extra long to get the taste out of my mouth.

I flick off the light and open the bathroom door gently so I do not wake up Mama. I could probably play a set of bagpipes without waking her, but I move quietly anyway. A light from the city shines in through a window in the kitchen, and I hear the faint noise of a siren as I get a plastic cup from the cupboard and fill it with tap water. I don't know why sirens make me feel safe but they do. They probably should make me feel unsafe as it means the police are probably on their way to get some bad people.

I hear Mama snore; I set my cup of water down on the kitchen table without taking a drink. I make my way to the living room and carefully pull her shoes off and put them against the wall so if she wakes up to go to the bathroom in the middle of the night she won't trip over them. I keep a blanket in the corner for nights like this; I get it and cover her up. While I do all of this, she does not move a muscle or change her breathing one bit. I have done this so many times, I have lost track.

Back in the kitchen, I slowly sip my water. The clock on the wall reads three twenty-seven. I have to get up and go to school in a few hours, and now I am wide awake. As I look around the kitchen, I see that Mama left her bottle out. She usually hides it in the cabinet above the refrigerator or behind the icemaker in the freezer. It is not like it is a big secret or anything, but she tries to hide it as best she can. One time, when she left her bottle out, I dumped it all in the sink. Somehow she remembered it was not empty and she wore me out the next day when I got home. She told me I was just wasting money and she asked me if I would burn a ten dollar bill. I said I was sorry and that I would never do it again. I decided, on that very day, that you can't make people quit something they don't want to quit. So, I make sure the lid is screwed on tight and I hide the bottle behind the icemaker in the freezer.

As I shut the freezer door, I hear footsteps blaze across the living room, and I hear the bathroom door being thrown open. I crane my neck and see Cecil hovering over the toilet, just as I was, minutes before. I wet a hand towel and squeeze it out so it is nice and damp. As he continues to heave, I gently place it on his forehead which is burning up and sweaty. He glances up at me, and I can tell he is glad to see me.

"I was here doing the same thing about twenty minutes ago," I tell him in between his heaves. "Keep that

49

towel for your head or to wipe your mouth, and I will get you a glass of ice water."

Cecil nods his head in pain and somehow mutters, "Thanks."

When I return to the bathroom, the smell is awful and I reach over Cecil's shoulder and flush the toilet. He is still poised over the toilet, but I think he might be finished as I can tell his body has relaxed and his breathing is returning to normal. He still has the hand towel on his forehead, so I pull a washcloth out from under the sink and wet it for his mouth.

Handing it to him I say, "Wipe your mouth, bro."

Cecil cusses and turns to sit on the floor. I take the washcloth that he has just used to wipe his mouth and hand him the cup of ice water. He takes it and begins to gulp.

"Slow down!" I command. "Drink it slowly," I say again with a gentler tone. "Just a little bit. Let your stomach get used to that before you give it more." I let him take another sip and then take the cup from him. "Splash some water in your face and brush your teeth," I command. "I did after I threw up and it made me feel much better. I'll take your water into the kitchen."

After helping Cecil off the floor, I leave him in the bathroom. As I leave, he is splashing his face with water and staring at himself in the mirror just as I did. I can tell by his expression that he is shocked by what he sees.

I set his cup of water across from mine at the kitchen table and wait for him. If he is anything like I was twenty minutes ago, he is exhausted. A few moments later, he stumbles into the kitchen and plops down in the kitchen chair across from mine.

"You just did that too?" he asks.

"Yep," I answer. "I'm pretty sure it was the hot dogs."

"Don't even say that word," he winces. "That was it. Where did those come from?"

"Mama brought them home," I say.

"I hope she didn't get them from the Oasis Grocery," Cecil says.

"We told her not to buy anymore meat from there," I answer. "Remember the sausages she bought there?"

"Don't remind me."

"I don't know why she would go there?" I wonder out loud.

"I do," Cecil answers.

"Why?"

"It has to do with her 'special drinks' as she calls them."

"OK, what?" I ask.

Cecil sighs like he is about to tell me the world really is flat. "You know how we get food stamps from the government?" Cecil asks hesitantly.

"Yeah," I say. "I've seen the food stamps."

"Mama trades them at the Oasis Grocery."

"What do you mean, she trades them? You are supposed to trade them for food, right?"

Cecil sips his water. "In a perfect world you are, Mash. We don't live in a perfect world."

"Then what does she trade them for?" I ask.

"I can't believe I am going to tell you this," Cecil says.

"Tell me," I beg.

"OK," he says. "I'll tell you, but you can't tell her you know. You know it won't change anything."

"I won't tell her," I say. "I know how she is."

"OK," Cecil concedes. "Mama goes to the Oasis Grocery and gives the cashier a ten dollar food stamp and they give her a five dollar bill in return."

"But she loses five dollars," I say perplexed.

"You can't buy special drinks with food stamps," Cecil announces. "You need cash, bro."

"How could she?" I ask the night.

If this was not enough bad news for one night, Cecil continues with one more piece of disturbing information. "In an unspoken way of thanking the Oasis

Grocery, she does a little shopping there with some of her other food stamps. And I am guessing if the employees are crooked with their food stamps, they must be crooked with other things, such as the expiration dates of meat."

"I can't believe the world is such a terrible place," I say. Something about the night makes things seem worse than they really are. As I sit at the kitchen table with Cecil, I feel worried and scared. I hear another siren; I get up from the table and walk back to my bedroom.

As I walk past Mama on the couch, I look at her with anger for the first time in my life. She has disappointed me, confused me, saddened me, worried me, and a whole lot of other things—this is the first time she has made me feel angry—and I feel like I could tear down the whole city with my bare hands.

Chapter 12

I wake up about thirty minutes before my alarm and puke my guts out. I am not going to school today. I bring the kitchen trash can beside my bed and settle in for the day. I doze in and out until nine o'clock. At nine o'clock Mama wakes up.

She always screams for Clarence when she wakes up. She pops up off the couch and screams his name and punches at the sky. I don't know who Clarence is, but he must be the end all.

Mama falls off the couch, as she usually does, and lies flat as expected for a few seconds on the floor, staring at the ceiling. Reality always comes back to her after a moment or two. She will get up, and I can always tell if it is going to be a good or bad day for me by what she does next. She will either go straight into the bathroom and take a shower, which means it will be a good day to be with her. Or, she will go into the kitchen and put ice cubes in a glass, which means it will be a bad day to be around her. I have always pondered how she decides every morning what she will do. I have wondered if it is a feeling she has, or a thought with which she cannot deal. I make an instant decision that if she goes into the kitchen for ice, I am going to ask her about it today. If not, I am going to ask her who Clarence is. Either way, it is going to be an exciting morning for me at home.

Without noticing I am even home, she walks into the bathroom and shuts the door. I feel nervous as I hear the water run in the tub. The hot and cold taps squeak and moan as Mama twists them on. The sound changes as she pulls the knob that makes the water shoot out of the shower head instead of in the tub, and I hear her pull the shower curtain closed with a clattering of the shower rings across the old rod.

While she is in the shower, I take the chance to see if Grandma or Cecil are home. I don't want them to get in the way of my plan of asking Mama about Clarence. I tiptoe into the living area and see that both Grandma's and Cecil's doors are open. Both of their beds are empty. So far so good.

I go back to my bed and pull up the covers, still hearing the water running in the shower. I think for a minute that I hear singing. I wonder if Mama will notice I am home when she gets out of the shower. I am sure she won't ask me why I am not at school. As I hear the water being turned off, I try to decide if I will even tell her I am sick. She is not the best caretaker and when I'm sick it usually just makes her feel guilty. She feels guilty that she doesn't want to spend money on medicine, and she feels guilty that we don't have insurance and on and on. So, usually when I get sick, I try to hide it from her.

Mama comes out of the bathroom in her robe and I cough once just to let her know she is not alone in the apartment. After I do this, I close my eyes and lie very still as if I am sleeping. I hear her footsteps near my room and slowly open my eyes as if I am just waking up.

"Hey baby," she says as she walks into my room. "Why do you have the trash can by your bed?" she asks.

I am surprised she noticed. "I got sick a couple of times during the night," I say. "Cecil did too," I add. "We think it was the hot dogs."

"You and Cecil told me not to trust that meat from the Oasis Grocery," she says. "I won't buy there no more," she promises.

"Will you sit down here for a minute?" I ask, patting a place on the edge of my bed.

"Of course, baby," she answers. "What's on your mind?"

"Don't get mad, Mama," I begin, "but I gotta know something."

"What's that," she says with a concern I have never seen in her face.

"Who is Clarence?"

She coughs and nervously wipes her palms and fingers across her face as she looks out the window. I can tell she is thinking, and I stay still and quiet and let her think.

"Your daddy," she finally answers.

I wait for more as I look into her face that has gone completely sad.

"I'm sorry I asked, Mama," I offer.

"No, baby," she says. "I am sorry it took so long for me to tell you."

"Does he live here in the city?" I ask.

Mama begins to cry silent tears. She wipes her tears with both hands and trembles slightly. I put my hand on her knee and squeeze just a little to let her know I am here.

"He did before he died," she answers.

I am not too surprised to hear this answer. I have fantasized for years about my father. In some of my fantasies he was dead. In my dead dreams of him he had been a war hero, fireman, police officer, or some type of guy who helped other people. Sometimes he was an artist, an inventor or a musician. Sometimes I imagined he was just a guy who worked at a gas station or some other boring job and he got real sick and died.

Before now, I had always wished he was alive. In the worst of moments, I imagined him in jail or too tied down with work to call or write. Maybe he was lost at sea or had amnesia. And now I know for sure; he is dead.

"Was he a good man, Mama?"

Without missing a beat she answers, "No."

I wait for her to tell me why and she just stares at the table.

"Does Cecil know about him?" I ask.

"Yes," she answers. "I figured you would have asked Cecil about your daddy by now."

"I *have* asked," I say. "He always swears he doesn't know anything." I watch her and she continues to stare into the table. I don't know if she is trying to decide what to tell me or where to start the story or if she is trying to block the whole thing out.

She lifts her head and looks at me directly in the eyes. She rarely looks me in the eyes, so I know she is dead serious.

"Your daddy was a hustler. Never had a real job, but stayed busy acting like he was working on making a million dollars. When he did have a little money, he acted like it wouldn't ever go away and just about spent it faster than he could take it out of his pocket. That man made so many promises he didn't keep and told me so many lies. I sometimes don't even know what is the truth about him and what is a story. But, in 1995, before you were born, the Atlanta Braves were in the World Series. They won it that year and the whole city was on fire with Braves fever. Tickets to the baseball games were hard to come by and people were buying them for hundreds of dollars. Your daddy had a partner he hung around who had the idea of making fake tickets and selling them on the street. His friend had some other friends who had computers and printers that could make tickets look exactly like the real ones. For every one your daddy sold, he got to keep half the money. He made a killing. Once the police found out about the scam, he did the smart thing and laid low. He went to live with his mama in Florida for almost a year. When he came back, the money of course was gone, and he worked other little scams making a little cheese here and there.

"When you were born in 1999, he promised to go straight and I actually believed him. He got a job at a car wash and worked pretty steady for nearly six months. In January of 2000, the Super Bowl between the Saint Louis Rams and the Tennessee Titans was played in Atlanta at the Georgia Dome, and your dad's old partner came around talking about the ticket scam again. His partner told him the World Series money was chump change compared to what they would make on a Super Bowl. It didn't take long before he talked your daddy into the scam; tickets to Super Bowls go for thousands of dollars. Your daddy was in and he got greedy. Once again, the deal was he could keep half the money. He kept it all! He went down to his mama's in Florida again thinking it would pass over and he would get to keep all the money, but it didn't happen that way. The bosses of the operation went down there and found him and shot him in his own mother's kitchen."

As soon as Mama finishes, she gets up, opens the freezer, pulls out her bottle, skips the whole part of putting ice cubes in a glass and all that and drinks straight from the bottle.

Part IV

Juniper awoke to hear a wild thrashing noise. It was Junior's birthday and he had bought her a Pomeranian puppy, which he had put in the garage for the night. Rising from his bed, he guessed she had heard the puppy whining or barking and had discovered it. She was wild with joy as he entered the living room. Junior spun round and round with the little pup, and her feet danced in what reminded Juniper of a Snoopy dance.

"Happy birthday little sister," Juniper piped as he entered the room.

Junior stopped spinning and put the puppy down to the floor and attacked Juniper with a massive hug. She squeezed him until it almost hurt and said thank you over and over again and again in his ear.

"What are you going to name him?" Juniper asked.

"Booger," Junior answered without delay. "His name is Booger. Booger and me's going to be the best friends."

"I thought I was your best friend," Juniper teased.

"You were," Junior answered. "Sometimes you are too busy for me," she said picking up Booger.

"Don't you think Booger is kind of a weird name for a dog?" Juniper asked.

"Junior is a weird name for a girl," she answered seriously. "A girl with a weird name needs a dog with a weird name. We go together like peanut butter and ketchup."

"Most people would think a peanut butter and ketchup sandwich was disgusting."

"My point exactly."

"What?" Juniper asked.

"Don't you have something to do in your studio big brother?"

"I think I do. I will leave you and Booger alone. I am taking you out to your favorite restaurant later. OK?"

"Can Booger come?"

"We will talk about it later."

As Junior walked out the back door, he heard Junior giving the dog a command, and he could have sworn she said, "Motel!"

Inside the studio, Juniper plopped down in his recliner and grabbed the remote control and tuned the television to a twenty-four hour news station. The world, he thought, was going mad. He could not watch for too long or it would make him angry how ignorant some people were. The amount of hate in the world hurt his heart, and he changed the channel. The next channel he watched was about a documentary inside a prison. For some reason these shows mesmerized him. Even though he had watched hours upon hours of these types of shows, Juniper still wondered what it would actually be like to be locked up without his freedom.

The new scheme he was brewing up was daring, and he wondered if he might end up in prison because of it. He tried to think of all the crimes he might be accused of because of it—criminal mischief, vandalism... Was it worth it? The world needed some fun, he thought. *I'm not going to hurt anybody. I'm just going to make a splash. Make the headlines. Make people wonder who did this and why. It will take peoples' minds away from the craziness of the world and let them ponder art for a while. Art is important. Art is good. Art can save the world!*

After his pep talk to himself, Juniper decided he would like to play with clay. One of the best parts of being an artist was that an artist is never too old to play. The ceramic section of his studio was enclosed and sealed off from the rest of the studio. With clay comes dust, and dust floats and travels. If the clay area was not separated from the rest of the studio, the clay dust would find its way into paintings and absolutely everything else in the room. All the nooks and crannies would be filled with clay dust, and

Juniper had learned this the hard way years ago. The clay section of the studio was separated by huge glass panels Juniper designed and installed so he would not feel isolated from the heart of the studio when he was working with clay.

Juniper hit play on a button just inside the door, and the music of Bill Withers filled the room. Music played an important role in Juniper's studio and in his life. Music took his mind to fantastic places his body would never go. Music, Juniper thought, had the ability to bring back memories, wake him up, pump him up, calm him down, and put him to sleep. Through music he was able to feel indescribable thrusts of energy, power to take his mind to the next level, and the delicate balance the world and his emotions teetered on. He felt there were secrets hidden between the notes. He liked all styles of music but tended to gravitate toward music from decades past. Most new music, he thought, lacked depth.

Juniper pulled up his sleeves and put on a ball cap he kept hanging on a hook next to the window. It was a Cleveland Browns hat he had bought just for the clay studio. The hat was brown and did not hide the dust as he thought it might. He tucked his hair underneath and kicked off his shoes. Juniper pulled off his socks and tossed them into a corner. Something about working with earth made him want to be barefooted. Juniper wriggled his toes and he was ready.

Bags of different types of clay sat around the room, and Juniper grabbed his favorite white raku clay. It didn't look white now, but after it was fired in the kiln it would be ivory white and ready for glaze. In his mind, Juniper saw a page from a Dr. Seuss book he remembered from childhood. From what he remembered, the whozits or whatzits were scrambling around the page, swinging and jumping and moving this way and that. But what he remembered most of all were the structures in the background. One might call them buildings, but they weren't exactly that. Nothing was exactly *that* or what one might think it *was* in a Dr. Seuss book. Juniper wanted to create one of these "buildings."

From what he remembered and saw in his mind, the structures were very tall, slender, and had a slight back and forth curve to them. The windows were all different, of course. Juniper visualized the final product in his mind. The body of the clay would be streaked with different textures, some gouged by his thumb and others with his fingers used like a cat clawing an object from top to bottom. The colors he saw in his mind were different shades and tints of red. Some of the reds would be dark and angry and others light and airy. Clouds of white would also float across the surface of the finished product.

After wedging the clay, Juniper used a roller made from a piece of pvc pipe to flatten the pieces called slabs. In order for the large slabs to be able to stand, they needed time to dry. With a little help from fans and lamps, Juniper could easily speed up the process and have the slabs ready in forty-five or so minutes. Juniper worked on the base and the roof while he waited. As he worked, he noticed movement in the yard outside of his studio window and stood still for a moment to watch his baby sister run around with her new dog, Booger. He smiled.

After completing the roof and the base, Juniper checked on the slabs and found them to be leather hard. With the help of some liquid clay called slip and a few other tricks, he quickly put the pieces together as he had envisioned. Once together, he softened up the parts he wished to bend by spraying them heavily with a hand sprayer set on mist and pushed his fist from the inside, bending the clay in the ways he desired.

Two hours later, one step of the ceramic process was finished. The next part was the hardest. The waiting. Before Juniper could do anything else he had to wait a week or probably two for the entire piece to be bone dry. The use of fans or lamps would not help but only make cracks and uneven, unnatural drying. Juniper lightly draped a sheet of plastic over the clay so it would not dry too fast, hung his hat on its hook, and walked out of the ceramic part of the studio.

Deciding Junior would soon be hungry, Juniper turned out the studio lights and headed to the house for a shower. Junior ran across the yard in front of him as Booger tried to chase her on his teeny tiny legs. Suddenly stopping, she turned around and yelled, "Motel!" Junior looked at Juniper with pride. "See, she already knows one command."

"But you said 'motel' didn't you?" Juniper asked.

"I decided I would have secret commands that only I know. And maybe I will tell you if you are nice to me."

"I'm always nice to you."

"OK. You're right. You're pretty nice most of the time. So guess what motel means?"

Looking bewildered, as was often the case when one had a conversation with Junior, Juniper said, "I guess it means stay because Booger isn't moving."

"Yes! Do you get it?"

"No."

Junior looked at him like he was a dope. "You *stay* in a motel. Duh."

"Well, excuse me. I am going to go take a shower and then I will take you anywhere you would like to go out to eat since it is your birthday."

"Can we go to Red Lobster and get lobster, fried shrimp, and that cheese bread stuff?"

"Of course."

"Can Booger come?"

"No."

"Why don't we go to Peking Palace then?" Junior suggested. "The lady that works there looks like she likes dogs."

"I assure you she does not want one in her restaurant."

"I got it!" Junior screamed, startling Booger. "We will go to the Dixie Drive-In where you pull up your car and each car has its own menu thingy hanging there by the place you park. All we have to do is push that button and the people inside will ask us what we want, and then they will bring it to us in the car. Perfect. You think you are the genius in this family, but it's really me. Can Booger go there? Please?"

"Great idea," Juniper answered. "I'll even buy Booger a hot dog."

"Foot long?"

"If you'll clean up the throw up later."

"Deal."

Chapter 14

Inside the secret recording studio, atop the King Cone building Stuart hit stop on his mega computer's audio system. He smiled a great smile feeling he had just recorded a brilliant track. It was part of a song he wrote about something he thought would happen in his future that would give him a reason to keep going. To an outsider, it probably looked as though Stuart had it all. He had a great job, he was rich, good looking, and incredibly personable. Underneath it all he was quite sad. Something was missing.

He exited the building without being noticed and started walking down the sidewalk without really thinking about where he was going. He walked aimlessly for thirty or so minutes when his tummy began to rumble. It was nearly dark and Stuart remembered he had not eaten all day. His nose smelled burger grease and it led him around the block to a small diner.

Inside the diner, he took a red stool at the counter and through a paneless window he watched the man in the kitchen flip a couple burgers. His stare caught the man's attention, and he received a nod of acknowledgement. The man walked toward him, and Stuart realized he had not looked at the menu.

"What can I get for you, young man?" the cook asked.

"I smelled those burgers from around the corner," Stuart answered. "I am going to have to have one of those."

"I have ten different varieties," the cook said. "Have you had a chance to look at the menu?"

"No."

"Can I offer a suggestion?"

"Please."

"You look like you would devour the Smoke House Fire BBQ Burger."

"Sounds delicious," Stuart drooled.

"Two delicious beef patties, homemade secret award winning barbeque sauce, thick sliced bacon, thin sliced jalapeño peppers, lettuce, home grown tomato, and your choice of cheese, all delivered on an onion roll I baked this morning."

Stuart almost fell off his stool. Before doing so, he was able to give the cook a thumbs up.

"Fries or onion rings?" the man asked.

"Both," Stuart gulped in his delirium.

The cook laughed all the way back to the kitchen. Stuart watched him pull the burgers off the grill that had finished cooking and start his order. As the meat hit the heated grill it sizzled and smoke gently rose from around its pink circumference. The cook dressed the burgers as if he had done it his entire life and Stuart smiled at his expertise. Being an excellent business man himself, Stuart knew a pro when he spotted one.

When his burger arrived, Stuart had to restrain himself from pouncing on it like a wild dog. He was not sure how he was going to get his mouth around the creation. He thought it looked like a picture in a magazine or something he might see on one of the food channels on television. The onion rings were still popping and the cook assured him they were Vidalia onions.

Stuart attacked the burger, and it was to die for. The cook brought him a medium sized saucer filled with ketchup, and he altered dunking the fries and the onions rings into the red sauce trying to decide which were better. For the first few minutes of his eating adventure, he stared only at his plate and the food. Once some of the food reached his stomach and he relaxed, he looked up again at the diner and the cook. Stuart felt something special. He wondered if the food was making him giddy with such pleasant thoughts and feelings about a place that in reality was quite plain.

"Can I get you a refill?" the cook asked, picking up Stuart's glass of iced tea.

"Please," Stuart answered. He watched as his glass filled with some of the best tasting iced tea that had ever crossed his lips. "May I ask your name?"

"Of course you can. My name is Henry Johnson, but most folks call me Mr. Henry."

"Mr. Henry," Stuart said aloud as if he were hearing his voice for the first time.

He did not want to tell Mr. Henry his real name as everybody in the city knew Stuart King was the head of King Cone, so he said, "My name is Billy. Billy Green."

The two men shook hands as Mr. Henry eyed him suspiciously.

"Can I ask you another question, Mr. Henry?"

"Absolutely."

"Who owns this place?"

"I do," Mr. Henry answered.

"I thought so. I can tell by the way you hold yourself. Can I ask you one last question?"

"Of course," Mr. Henry answered. "I have nothing to hide," he said with a wry smile.

"Do you own this building?"

"Yes I do."

"You must be aware of the fact that you could sell this plot of land for millions upon millions of dollars," Stuart said.

"I know that, Mr. Green. I was once offered twenty-seven million dollars for this piece of land and I declined."

"Why?"

"What is a man like me going to do with twenty-seven million dollars?" Mr. Henry asked with a laugh.

"You could do whatever you would like," Stuart answered.

"I like cooking," Mr. Henry answered, looking dead into Stuart's eyes. "I don't need anything more than what I already have to do that. I guess I could open a big fancy restaurant with fountains and shiny things and have a wait staff in tuxedos and valet parking. That is not me though. This is me," he said, holding his hands up.

Stuart looked around and took in all that Mr. Henry had just said.

"What do you love to do?" Mr. Henry asked.

Stuart felt like a kid visiting Santa when he answered timidly, "I like to make music."

"Then find a way to make music. Work a cruddy paying job so you can come home after work and pick up your instruments and make your music. Work at a music store, maybe. If it is that important to you, you will find a way."

"I play the acoustic guitar," Stuart confessed.

"Dinner is free if you promise to come by some day and play me a song on said guitar."

Stuart realized his plate was empty. "I'll do it, Mr. Henry."

"You do that, Mr. Whatever your real name might be." Mr. Henry gave Stuart a playful wink and walked back into the kitchen.

Stuart walked back to the parking garage next to his office. He strolled slowly, thinking about all of the things Mr. Henry had said. Stuart could barely believe that Mr. Henry could have sold his plot of land for twenty-seven million dollars. Mr. Henry did not need the money to be happy. Stuart thought of all the luxuries in his life that had made him happy for some time. He climbed into his black Lexus and started the engine. They were not making him happy anymore, and he could not understand it.

At his home in a city north of Atlanta named Alpharetta, he parked the Lexus in the four car garage, which happened to be full. He owned one of the biggest and most tricked out trucks a person has ever seen, which had a dirt bike strapped in the back. Next to that was a red sports car that probably cost more than the average family makes in two or three years of working. In the final spot sat two motorcycles, a Ducati for speed and a Harley for cruising. None of these possessions excited him the way they used to.

Walking into the house he activated the voice commanded lights by saying, "Lights on." Stuart had the system wired to turn on every single light in the entire house at this command, even the lights in the closets. He felt less lonely with all of the lights on. In the living room, he said, "TV on," and the television came alive. "ESPN," he said next, and the television switched itself to the requested channel. Stuart walked out of the room. The sound of the television made it feel like someone was in the house with him, and he liked that feeling.

Stuart's house would be better described as a mansion. It had eleven bedrooms, thirteen bathrooms, two game rooms, an outdoor *and* indoor pool, basketball court, tennis court, two-lane bowling alley, state-of-the-art kitchen, and a few other bells and whistles that would make the average man or woman green and sick with envy.

Stuart wandered aimlessly through the house for over an hour. He gathered all the balls on his billiards table, racked them and decided not to play. He looked through all of his Wii, Play Station 3, and X-Box games and found that nothing interested him. He perused his DVD collection. He tested the waters of the indoor and the outdoor pools with his toes. He tested the waters in the outdoor whirlpool. Stuart eyed the basketball goal and thought of shooting a few hoops. None of these things stirred his insides.

Feeling empty, Stuart tried to think of what he would like to do and what might make him happy. He thought of two things—people and music. For a minute, he played with the idea of breaking the pump for the pool or flooding the washing machine so he could call in the couple that took care of his home and the surrounding grounds, but finally decided he could not do that to Mr.

69

and Mrs. Vargas on their day off. They were wonderful people, and Stuart decided he would not feel right deceiving them just to ease his loneliness.

Mr. and Mrs. Vargas started working for him after his last housekeeper of fifteen years quit abruptly saying she could not put up with his moodiness and depression any longer. Her husband, who had kept the grounds, left with her, although he confessed to Stuart that he understood feeling low and did not want to leave, but had to choose between his wife and his job.

The King Cone Corporation owned a piece of a lot of things and one of its ventures led to Stuart's hiring of Mr. and Mrs. Vargas. A business friend of Stuart, named Gary Slidell, had employed Mr. and Mrs. Vargas to run a dining hall while he worked on one of his projects. Once the project ended, the couple was out of a job. Mr. Slidell happened to know they were looking for work at the same time Stuart mentioned his housekeeper and maintenance man/groundskeeper had bolted. Mr. Slidell set up the interview and Stuart hired them on the spot. The Vargas family had a daughter named Cynthia and a son named Oscar. They came with their parents half of the time with Stuart's permission and he actually loved it when they were at his home. When they all were at his home, he imagined having a big family one day, and just the sound of all of their voices made him happier.

Most of Stuart's musical equipment was kept in the secret studio on the top floor of the King Cone building because work is where he spent the majority of his time, but he did have one acoustic guitar under his bed, in case a song idea came to him in the middle of the night. The thought of music sent a chill up his spine that nearly threw him to the ground. His heart started pumping, and his brain started to whirr. He had been holding a bowling ball, and he dropped it and ran.

The door to Stuart's room was wide open, and it was a good thing, as he ran into his bedroom and dove onto the bed, sliding across it to poke his head under its other side. His hand reached under and grabbed the handle to the case of his emergency guitar. He pulled it out and unclasped the locks holding the guitar close like a long lost friend. Stuart revved up the guitar and his fingers by strumming a few chords. His blood began to bubble. Holding the Takemine, a Japanese acoustic, he looked down the frets and back up again. He squeezed the capo perched atop the neck of the guitar and fastened it to the fourth fret. Stuart played an E minor chord, followed by a C and a D. He played them slowly at first, finding a rhythm, then his fingers took over the melody as he picked the chords with a simple tickle of each digit. He breathed in and out and once again felt like a real person.

Chapter 15

Juniper sat up in bed to the sound of Junior's frightened voice. His eyes glanced at the clock, which read four fifty in the morning. He knew at once she was talking in her sleep. Junior would oftentimes have nightmares. Juniper quickly rose from beneath his comfortable sheets and threw on a robe he kept next to his bed for this exact reason. He hurried to her room.

The noise had obviously not affected Booger as he slept soundly at the foot of her bed. Upon entering her room, he saw Junior thrashing about wildly and Booger's eye flew open with uncertainty. Juniper sat on the bed next to Junior and put his right hand on her back and his left brushed the sweat filled hair from her eyes.

Junior stopped flailing and breathed heavily as Juniper said, "Shhh," over and over with a gentle calming rhythm. "Shhh... Shhh... Shhh..."

Feeling his presence and snapping out of her dream, Junior opened her eyes, which were still wild with the dreaming world. She grasped whatever parts of Juniper she could, and held on like he might disappear at any moment.

"I was trapped," Junior said mostly with her breath.

"You're OK now," Juniper reassured her.

"I was in the middle of some woods, and the branches and vines just come on down and trapped me. I was gonna try and get out, but then thorns started popping out all over the place. I was looking everywhere for a way out and it kept getting darker and darker like it was gonna come up a fast rain storm or something. Then I decided I didn't care if I got all cut up and stuff, but I was gonna bust my way out of there and that's when I seen it. It was so awful, Juniper. Longest, ugliest, meanest snake you ever seen. I was so scared I couldn't even move and my plan of busting free just went up in smoke. I thought I was done for. I could hear Booger barking on the other side of the woods, and you was calling my name but I couldn't move."

"I'm here now," Juniper reassured her again. "I'll always be here for you."

"I don't like snakes," Junior commented.

"Me neither," Juniper answered.

"Why did God make snakes?"

"I don't know." Juniper smiled at her innocence. Changing the subject, he said, "I bet Booger has to go to the bathroom and we sure don't want him going on the carpet."

"Are you going back to bed?" Junior asked. "I'm too scared to go back and see that snake again."

"I guess we can go ahead and get up," Juniper answered. "I finished up the plans for our next art project and wanted to tell you about it anyway. You take Booger out to do his business and I will make some coffee."

Junior hopped out of bed and gave Booger one of her made up commands. "Boomerang," she said. Booger hopped off the bed and started to follow her down the hall. "Do you get it?" she called back to Juniper.

"No."

"A boomerang comes back to you. Boomerang means to come."

"Oh," Juniper said, "very clever."

Junior took Booger outside and Juniper made coffee. Coffee happened to be one of the many things Juniper spent a lot of money on, and he did not mind the hefty price tag because the product was primo. He had his coffee flown in from Hawaii. Hawaiian coffee was about the only coffee he would drink. His father only drank Hawaiian coffee. Juniper had never made this connection.

While the coffee was percolating, Juniper pulled out some photos he had previously assembled to present his art project idea to his sister. His heart skipped a few beats with excitement. He had previously thought the Death Valley Flower bloom was his masterpiece but was sure this one would replace it as his number one. This one would definitely be by far the riskiest art project he had ever contrived.

Junior and Booger came back in the house about the same time as the coffee was finished brewing. Junior did not drink coffee, so after Juniper poured himself a cup of the Hawaiian brew, he poured her a glass of chocolate milk. Junior liked to drink her chocolate milk in a coffee mug and pretend it was coffee. She had tried coffee on multiple occasions and had decided multiple times that it was awful. She could not understand why anyone would drink the stuff, and she especially could not understand why her brother could not begin his day until he ingested the terrible liquid. She did not understand a lot of things about her brother, but she loved him anyway.

Juniper held a coffee mug he had made, which happened to be his favorite, filled with the strong brew. He gave Junior her chocolate milk in her favorite mug and asked her to sit. She did as asked. He paced back and forth in front of her for a long minute before speaking. She was used to this, and it did not bother her in the least. Juniper would stop, sip his coffee and act as if he was about to speak, and continue pacing, going back to his thinking.

Finally he stopped, sipped, and actually spoke. "I've decided that you will not be a part of my next art project," he said solemnly. "I'm sorry, but I love you too much to put you in danger."

"That is fine," Junior answered. "I don't mind a bit."

"You don't?" Juniper asked.

"No. Not if you don't mind going to jail tomorrow."

"Why would I go to jail tomorrow?" Juniper asked, confused.

"Well," Junior began, "you will go to jail because buddy if I get cutted out of this project I will telephone call the Atlanta Journal, CNN, USA Today, and the New York Times, just to name a few of the papers and televisions I will call to tell them that you are the guy who did all of that crazy art stuff! Cut me out! Do it! Give me the phone."

"You would not do that to me," Juniper said.

"Yeah," she huffed. "And I thought you wouldn't ever be such a meany and kick me out of your project. If you do that to me I will do this to you," Junior threatened.

"Do you want to go to jail?" Juniper asked.

"You don't never go to jail," Junior answered.

"I might this time." Juniper paused and said, "How about this? I will tell you the idea and once you see how risky it is, you can make up your mind if you want to participate or not."

"Deal," she said.

Juniper pulled out the pictures and showed them to Junior as he finished his first cup of coffee.

Once she had viewed the photographs, Juniper said, "I am going to paint that."

Junior only said two things. She said, "You are crazy." She paused and scratched Booger behind his ear and also said, "I am in."

Part V

I throw up a couple more times before my stomach finally settles. Cecil comes running in from the corner store where he bought some Pepto Bismol and he heads straight to the bathroom. It seems as Cecil and I take turns talking to the porcelain. It is rare to see him get upset with Mama, but he really gives it to her for buying those hot dogs at the Oasis Grocery. Mama just takes it because after our talk about my daddy and her revealing what I have been wanting to know all these years, she has been sitting at the kitchen table enjoying one special drink after the other.

At about three thirty, my best friend Charles comes by to check on me.

"Ms. Monique sent a homework sheet for you," he says as he walks in the door. "She know you sick if you ain't at school. She said you love school. I know you do. What wrong with you?"

Charles can talk a mile a minute if you let him, and I think it is one of the reasons we are such good friends. He is a talker, and I am more of a listener.

"Mama bought some bad hotdogs at the Oasis Grocery," I say. "Cecil has been home all day too."

"Cecil stay home?" he says surprised. "Y'all must be sick as dogs for Cecil be staying home. Y'all mama should know better than buy meat at Oasis."

"She knows," I answer. "She doesn't care. She can be very selfish." She is right in the next room and I don't even care if she hears me.

"Straight up," Charles says. "Where she be now?"

"The kitchen," I answer.

Charles's eyes fly open and he flinches like he is about to get hit. "She gone come in here and kill you dead. Might get me on accident. You crazy?" His eyes stare toward the kitchen waiting for her to come around the corner.

"She's been real thirsty today."

"Oh," he answers. "Sorry."

Charles knows this means she has been having a lot of her special drinks.

"Are you feeling better?" Charles asks. "You look like you feeling better."

"Yeah," I answer. "I threw up my last time at about noon and ever since then I feel like myself again."

"Me and Daddy about to go over to Turner Field where the Braves play to hear a concert. I bet, I bet, I bet he ain't gonna mind none if you come on with us. You want to?"

"I don't have a ticket," I answer.

Charles laughs like I have just told the funniest joke he has ever heard. "We don't have tickets either," he says. "We just gone stand outside and listen. That be the beauty of a open air stadium concert. Don't need no ticket. Music floats right on out to the people on the street. Can't see nothing. That be true. You don't need to see music to enjoy it! Blind people like music. You coming?"

"Who is playing?" I ask.

"Stevie Wonder." He smiles. "He can't see the show either. He blind. Ain't that something. Me, you, Daddy, and Stevie Wonder gone see the same show of nothing and he the one playing. Life be so funny, don't it Mash? You coming or not?"

"I love Stevie Wonder. I'm coming," I answer.

"Good," Charles answers. "You don't want to see ole Stevie anyhow. He done got so fat you wouldn't even believe it be him. Can't blame him though. He don't know he fat. He can't look in no mirror and say to he self that he need to watch them Twinkies he be eating. He probably don't even know the difference between thin folks and fat folks. I bet he do like Twinkies, though. He just look like a Twinkie man."

"Why don't you stop talking for a minute and let's go," I say.

"Daddy says I talk a lot."

"You do."

We take the MARTA train over to Turner Field, and once we get there, I see almost as many white people as I see people like me. I guess white folks like Stevie Wonder too. He *is* good. All the white folks have tickets, though. I don't see any of them finding a comfortable spot to sit outside like us. We even brought an old quilt to sit on, and Charles's daddy bought a bag of roasted peanuts just like we were going to a ball game.

I start shelling some peanuts and before I know it, I hear a funky guitar picking out the notes to the song *Superstition*. The crowd inside the stadium goes wild, and we can hear just as good as it must sound inside. When Stevie Wonder thanks the crowd for coming, I can even see him smile, with his big black sunglasses hiding his broken eyes.

When he plays *You Are the Sunshine of My Life*, I lie on my back on the quilt and close my eyes. The song has saxophones in it and with my eyes closed, it seems as though the saxophone players are hovering above me and floating back and forth as if they were on clouds on top of waves. I feel warm inside, and for a minute, I forget where I live and who lives with me. I feel free.

A plane flies over, and the buzz of its engine tells my ears to open my eyes and they do. My eyes open to see a gigantic and beautiful plane above me. I love planes. I love everything about them. The lights, the wings , the metal, the engines, the noises they make. I love them.

"I see you looking at that plane," Charles says. "Why you like them ole flying machines anyways? If somebody come up and gave me plane tickets right now to go on over to China or Russia or even Miami, Florida, I would have to tell them to go on ahead and keep them tickets. I ain't getting myself that far off the ground in some ole machine. You know what I mean? Do they give all them folks traveling on they airplanes a parachute? I don't think so. What if they done ran out a gas? What if the guy who supposed to fill up the gas had a fight with his ole lady and be thinking about her and done forgot to fill up the plane with gas? Huh? What then?"

I didn't really know how to answer his ridiculous question so I just appeased him and said, "Well, I guess everybody dies."

"Yeah," he said. "That why I ain't ever gone fly nowhere."

I would never tell him, but I think a person like Charles who has a mama and a daddy should be a little bit smarter than he is.

"When I become a pilot, will you fly with me?" I ask.

I watch Charles as he mulls this over. "Long as you keep a good eye on the gas man," he finally answers. "Can I sit up front with you?"

"I don't know what the rules are yet, but I will ask when the time comes. Cecil doesn't believe that I'll ever be a pilot."

"Cecil dumber than me," Charles says.

"You're not dumb," I say, slapping him on the back.

"I'm no Albert Bernstein."

"You mean, Albert Einstein?"

"See?" he says. "See? I just proved it right there. I'm not a genius."

"Nobody ever accused you of being a genius. I could tell you how to seem smarter starting right now though."

"Wear a bow tie?" he kids.

"No. Stop all your ghetto talking."

"You saying you want me talk like white folk? I ain't white and I ain't talking like it."

"So, from what you are saying, I talk like a white person?"

"No, you talk fine cause you ain't all uppity and junk." Charles pauses to think. "I guess I could talk like you but I ain't you, I'm me, and I like me the way I is. I'm not planning on being no pilot like you, so I don't need a be talking all fancy. I be happy doing engine work on buses like Daddy do."

"You know you still have time to be anything you want to be if you try hard in school," I say.

"I want to be a bus mechanic," he states.

"Nothing wrong with that," I answer. I know he doesn't want to talk about this and I know from the times before that I have tried, that it is useless. Charles is happy with his life and even though I can't seem to understand not wanting better, I have to try. He is my best friend.

The concert ends and we take the MARTA train back to our part of the city. For all of the talking that Charles does, his daddy doesn't do hardly any at all. I have heard people describe someone as "a man of few words." He is a man of very, very, very few words. Charles's mama talks more than Charles does and the man probably can't get a word in even if he tried. I imagine he has just gotten used to talking inside of his head to himself. Or maybe they talk so much and fill his head with so many words that when they are not talking, he doesn't think at all and he fills his head with silence.

The man of very, very, very few words asks us in his deep voice, "Can I buy you fellas a dog or a slice a pie?"

The thought of a hot dog makes my stomach churn and Charles comes to my rescue saying, "Daddy, I thought I done toll you earlier Mash's mama bought they last dogs at Oasis? He don't even want to hear the word till a long time off." His daddy just nods like he does most of the time instead of speaking. "Windy City make a good pie and you can order a whole pie or by the slice. How bout Windy City y'all?"

We both nod in agreement. Charles's daddy calls pizza, pie. He is from Chicago and supposedly people in that city call their pizzas by the name pies. I'll probably fly there one day and while I am in the city I think I will try some of their pie.

The inside of the Windy City is decorated with stuff from the Chicago Cubs, the Chicago Bears, and the Blackhawks. All of the televisions are tuned to stations from Chicago. On the wall, I see pictures of the Sear's Towers, Barack Obama, slices of pizza that look out of this world and the Chicago skyline. The booths are made of red brick with shiny black padded seats. The tabletops are glass and underneath are more Chicago memorabilia.

We all slide into a booth, and our waiter greets us immediately with menus. The menus are shaped like kites. Chicago, really is not known for kites, but it is known for being windy so I get the connection. For a pizza restaurant there is a lot of stuff on the menu. The list of toppings for the pizzas catch my eye immediately as it takes up half a page. Aside from the toppings I am used to seeing for pizza, at this place you can get broccoli, spinach, scrambled eggs, steak, fried mozzarella, shrimp, crab, potato, green tomatoes, buffalo wing something-or-other, maple sugar, and you name it and the restaurant might just have it. Some of the stuff you can get on a pizza here is just disgusting. A few on the list that seem nasty are escargot or snails, fish eggs or caviar, and quadruple mushroom surprise. If I had to eat a pizza made of those three things or jump into an active volcano, I would not even think twice and dive head first into the lava. In my opinion, your mama just raised you wrong if you like those things.

I order two slices. One with sausage and pineapple and the other with pepperoni and broccoli. I am curious how broccoli will taste on a pizza and how it will be cooked. I like broccoli and Mama almost never cooks it for us. Most of the vegetables we eat at our house are frozen and have lost a lot of their taste. A sentence at the bottom of the menu promises that everything is fresh and never frozen. I am excited about fresh broccoli. Wow! My life must be pretty dull to be excited about fresh broccoli.

Chicago pie takes a long time to bake. The waiter told us something about the special ovens and blah, blah,

blah. Bottom line, he said the long cooking time makes a better tasting pie. It seems like forever after he takes our order until we get the food. Charles talks the whole time about Stevie Wonder, girls, Ms. Monique, and the horrors of the Oasis Grocery. His daddy and I listen.

When the pie finally comes, it is as good as advertised or better. The broccoli on the pizza is crisp on the outside and tender on the inside. It is perfect. What started out as a pretty rough day, hearing about my dead daddy and throwing up hot dogs for hours, winds down into a pretty good day. Some days are funny like that.

Chapter 17

Grandma gives me a few dollars like she does every now and then and asks me if I can eat at Hog's for dinner. Her book club is coming over.

"What about Mama?" I ask. "Remember the time she ruined the meeting?"

"I don't think I'll ever forget it." Grandma laughs thinking about it. "It's funny now," she says. "It's so amusing how something can happen that is so awful and after time goes by it gets better."

I want to ask her about the car wreck and the time she was burned in the kitchen. I want to ask why those things never got better, but I don't.

"Mama gathered up all the books in the room and screamed something about white devils and threw all the books out the window. Amazing what a thirteen story fall can do to a book." Grandma laughs again. "Your mama was even more angry when I made her replace all those books. I think it cost her about eighty dollars. She almost lost her mind when I gave her the bill I wrote up."

"Mama was mad at you for almost a whole month," I remember aloud.

"When I told her the book club was coming over tonight, she stomped out the door and told me she would be back tomorrow when all the bookworms were gone."

"What book is your club reading?"

"A book titled *The Help*."

"What's it about?" I ask.

"Well," she says, trying to think of where to start. "I know you have learned all about desegregation and how it used to be for black folks a long time ago." She pauses and I nod. "The book is set in Mississippi in a time right before Martin Luther King Jr. comes on the scene and shakes up the whole South. It's about black maids working for white ladies and a white lady who sympathizes with them and wants to write a book about it."

"It sounds good."

"Oh, it is. Brought back a lot of memories," she says as she watches for my reaction to her statement."

"You worked as a maid for a white lady?" I ask.

"Yes sir," she answers. "Mrs. Jean Hammond."

"Did she treat you right?" I ask.

"Most of the time," she answers. "But I knew she didn't think of us as being equal. She loved me, but she loved me like you love a dog. You know a dog is not on your level but you have a lot of love for it. People were just like that back then and sometimes I think it wasn't their fault. Their mothers and fathers brought them up thinking black folks were different. Some problems take generations to fix."

"I can't imagine having to use a different bathroom or water fountain just because my skin pigment is dark," I say.

"But that is how it was, baby," she says. "I don't think you could have been a pilot back in those days. You are lucky to be living in the days you are living in."

"I was trying to tell that to Charles just last night," I say, so excited I am about to jump out of my skin. "We weren't having this exact same conversation, but it seems like he is stuck back in 1960 where all he can be is a bus mechanic. What kind of dream is that?" I ask.

"Some folks just haven't got it yet, baby," she says. "They will. They will."

I stand there and realize everything my grandma has been through in her life, and I am filled with love for her. I go over and hug her neck a little harder than I mean to. I kiss her cheek and head for the door. When my hand is on the door, she stops me.

"Remember, baby," she says. "Sometimes it takes generations to fix a problem."

I climb onto my favorite stool at Hog's. One of the things I love about Mr. Henry is that when I need work he treats me like an employee, and when I have money he

85

treats me like a customer. As I get settled on the stool, he hands me a menu, and a twinkle flashes behind both of his eyes.

"Don't need it, do you?" he says.

"No, sir," I answer. "Let me think a minute, though," I say. "I do know I want water to drink."

Mr. Henry walks to the kitchen to get my glass of water, and I take inventory of the customers in the restaurant. There is an old man drinking coffee and reading the newspaper. Two younger ladies are chatting over lemon meringue pie. Mr. Henry sets the glass of water in front of me and pulls his order book out of his apron, ready to write.

"Ten hot wings, extra hot, with celery and blue cheese dressing on the side. I would also like a side of curly fries."

"Mash," Mr. Henry starts. "The last time you had the extra hot wings you had tears pouring out of your face and onto my counter. We could have hooked a bag up to your nose and caught a gallon of snot."

"That's how you know they are good," I say.

"OK," he concedes. "One order of hot wings, one order of curly fries, and one thousand napkins coming up!"

As I eat, the diner fills up, and Mr. Henry stays busy with other customers. Every so often, he comes by the counter where I am seated to refill my glass and offer more napkins. When I am finished, he slides me a bill. I don't expect charity, and I am glad he does not give it. If he did, I would not come back. I pay my bill and leave a good tip and as I head for the door, he stops me.

"Judd was looking for you earlier," he says. "He said something about MARTA and a plan he had for you to get somewhere. Does that make sense?"

"Yes," I say. "Thanks, Mr. Henry." I sniff back a trail of snot that was trying to run out of my nose. "The wings were awesome."

Mr. Henry is cleaning my spot and picking up my tip when he looks up at me and says, "No, Mash. You are awesome."

I swear Mr. Henry is wiping a tear from under his eye as I leave.

I enter Art Inkorporated and hear the familiar buzzing sound of the tattoo needles filling the air. Gina is at the front desk and motions for me to go on back to Judd's area. Judd has what I call a poser in his chair. He is young, white, and wearing a black skull cap. The look he is trying to pull off doesn't match the Lexus key I spot sitting on a table with his iPhone. The tattoo in progress confuses me even more. It reads, "Save the Earth" and Judd is adding details to what looks like what will be the earth spinning out of control with a tornado effect surrounding it. An outline of a whale, a cut down tree, and an oil rig have beginning outlines flying from the tornado lines. It is a very large tattoo on the guy's back and one I am sure he will regret later. I can't help but share my confusion with a look I give Judd when he pauses for a moment to look at me. The guy receiving the tattoo is not looking, and Judd raises his shoulders and eyebrows relaying to me without words that he is just as confused as I am about the guy. The guy looks like a grungy townie, and his tattoo makes it seem like he is a hippy? I can smell his cologne and none of the clues I am gathering about him go together. Some weird people come into this place!

"Did you just eat those fire hot wings at Hog's?" Judd asks.

"How do you know that?" I ask.

"You don't seem sad, but it looks like you have been crying for hours. Your nose is running like a faucet, and your eyes are puffy. How can that be enjoyable?"

"It is," I assure him. "I can still taste them and smell them and feel them."

"You gonna feel them later as well, if you know what I mean."

"Mr. Henry said you had figured out a plan for me to take on MARTA."

"I did," Judd answers. "Look under my hat on my desk. I think that's where I left what I wrote down for you."

I pick up his Atlanta Braves hat and find a torn piece of notebook paper under it, with detailed directions on how to take the public transit from our neighborhood to the Peachtree Dekalb Airport. Bingo! I'm on my way!

Chapter 18

Stuart awoke to the smell of coffee. He quickly sat up, confused, as he was certain he did not make any coffee. A steaming cup of coffee sat on his night stand next to his bed. As he sat up, he realized he was not in his pajamas, but he was still wearing his clothes from the day before. Before he could think about the situation anymore, Mrs. Vargas walked into the room and pulled the curtains away from the wide window that overlooked the backyard and the magnificent outdoor pool.

"I am sorry if I woke you and you were planning to take the day off," she said, "but I have never seen you take the day off before and just figured that you overslept."

"I don't really remember falling asleep," Stuart said, as he picked up the coffee cup.

"I found you asleep this morning, snoring like a bear, with your arms wrapped around a guitar." Mrs. Vargas cracked a smile at him. "I rescued the guitar and put it back in its case. You were drooling all over it and I was afraid you might somehow break it."

"Wow!" Stuart said. "Thanks. I was feeling very sad last night for some reason and I found solace in my guitar. I remember strumming it with my eyes closed. I must have fallen asleep while doing that."

"I don't want to overstep my bounds," Mrs. Vargas said, "but I can't help thinking something that I have wanted to say for a while now."

"You can say it," Stuart assured.

"You have this wonderful house and a great job and so many incredible possessions." Mrs. Vargas paused, unsure of whether she should go on with her advice or not.

"Go on," Stuart said.

So she did. "Life is meant to be shared with other people. Life is meant to be enjoyed. I watch you work and work and work and you never seem to enjoy all the magnificent things you own. I have never seen you invite anybody over to visit or to have a party or dinner or anything. I have rarely seen you smile." Mrs. Vargas paused again, wondering, but then not caring if she was overstepping her bounds. "You were smiling this morning as you held the guitar." A smile crossed her face. "The guitar is special to you."

"It is," Stuart said. "I have a lot of ideas for songs, but I need some help with lead guitar and drums and things like that."

"I have a nephew named Emilio who drives a liquid tanker truck for a living, but his passion in life is music. He can play the lead guitar like any of the best guitarist of all time. He is amazing. He has a gift from God. He can listen to a song on the radio and play along like he was in the band. He is just so incredible."

"Where does he live?" Stuart asked.

"When we moved to Alpharetta, he moved in with us, and he now lives in Roswell. I can give you his number if you want to play with him sometime."

"I would like that," Stuart said. "I would like that a lot."

"Would you like me to find a suit for you to wear today?" Mrs. Vargas asked.

"I don't think so," Stuart answered. "I am not going to work today. I am calling in sick." Stuart smiled to the surprised look in Mrs. Vargas's eyes. "Please make me some more coffee. I think I am going to drink coffee by the pool for a few hours with my guitar, and then I would like to have lunch by the pool with two very important guests."

"What should I prepare?" Mrs. Vargas asked.

"It all depends," Stuart answered.

"Depends on what?"

"What is your favorite meal and Mr. Vargas's. You two are my guests."

Mrs. Vargas laughed like a school girl, covering her mouth as her eyes crinkled with giggles. "We will have authentic Mexican cuisine. I know for a fact that Emilio is off today. Should I invite him as well?"

Stuart's face lit up, and he said, "Please!"

Stuart stayed by the pool all morning. At times, he played the guitar. At times, he stared off into the clear blue sky, and every once in a while he got up and walked around the pleasant blue water of the pool and back to his coffee cup and guitar. Mrs. Vargas brought him a cinnamon roll that he did not eat. He said he was too excited about the lunch and meeting Emilio.

Mr. Vargas skimmed the pool for leaves as Stuart absent-mindedly strummed the guitar. Stuart stopped to watch Mr. Vargas and to pepper him with questions about Emilio.

"Is he really as good as Mrs. Vargas says he is?" Stuart asked.

"He is," Mr. Vargas answered.

"Does he like acoustic guitar? Does he like electric? Does he know how to play the harmonica? Can he sing harmony?" Stuart's questions were plentiful. One who didn't know he was the CEO of a very wealthy and powerful company would think he was a lost college kid looking for a buddy to go to a party.

Mrs. Vargas brought Stuart a large glass of ice water and took his coffee cup from him.

"I think you have had enough caffeine, Mr. King," she said. "Drink some water."

"Thanks," Stuart said, "and please call me Stuart."

The smells of cooking wafted out of the kitchen and onto the patio area where Stuart sat. Stuart pulled the aroma into his nose and looked to Mrs. Vargas with a smile. It smelled amazing, and he didn't realize how hungry he was until the moment the smell hit his brain. Stuart was now just as excited about the food as he was about the company.

"Oh my goodness," Stuart said. "That smells like heaven."

"It smells like the neighborhood I grew up in," Mrs. Vargas answered. "I hope you were not kidding when you said you would like authentic Mexican cooking."

"I don't usually joke around."

"Good. Because I have brought Acapulco to you. You are in for a real treat. If you would like to take a shower and get out of the clothes you were wearing yesterday, lunch will be ready in fifteen minutes."

Stuart did not realize that he was still in the clothes he had awaken in, the clothes of yesterday. He really did not care and felt comfortable in the clothes, but felt Mrs. Vargas was telling him in a round about way to go and shower up and change. Wanting to ultimately impress Emilio, he did as suggested and headed for the shower whistling along the way.

Chapter 19

Juniper dialed Nick's number on the special cell phone, and after going through the verbal codes to make sure the call was secure, he asked, "How is the search going?"

"Well, I have some very good news. Not only have I located a source for the perfect paint, but I have also made contact with a friend of mine who has access to a few different planes depending on your needs."

"Oh, that is great, great news. Tell me about the paint first. I assume you got the paint sample I mailed you so you could match my desired color?"

"I did," Nick answered. "My contact for the paint matched it exactly. He used to work for the government with Defense contractors and he knows all kinds of highly specialized and inventive people. The paint not only has the perfect coloring you requested, but it also has almost unimaginable adhesive properties. It is liquid, but the moment it makes contact with an object, it sticks and does not drip or splash back."

Juniper was laughing with anticipation and vision of how it would all play out. "You have done very well, my friend."

"My friend sent me a sample of the paint and you almost have to see it to believe how amazing it is. I took the gallon he sent me and dumped it on a concrete statue of a bulldog in my backyard, and none of it dripped to the ground. You will not believe this stuff."

"This sounds wonderful," Juniper said.

"I have even better news."

"I can't imagine what could be better than the news you have already given me."

"I was talking with my contact who is selling us the paint and asked him if he knew of any way to apply this paint very, very quickly. He just so happens to have a machine that will hold one hundred and ten gallons of the paint and somehow the machine forces the paint out at an incredibly quick speed."

"How quick is incredibly quick?" Juniper asked, now standing and pacing with excitement.

"Two and a half seconds."

"Two and a half seconds!" Juniper screamed. "Holy cow! Shazam! Bam! Ahhh!"

"I take it that the news makes you happy?" Nick joked.

"You have done very well, Nick."

"Thank you, sir."

"Remember how I told you I was going to pay you five times more than the Death Valley job?"

"Yes," Nick answered.

"Make it ten times the amount."

"Holy cow! Shazam! Bam! Ahhh!"

Juniper laughed. "I take it that makes you very happy?"

"Very happy," Nick said, "and I haven't told you about the planes yet."

"Oh yeah," Juniper said. "Tell me about the planes."

"You could not have picked a better day in the whole year to do this. On the same day you want to do this, the Peachtree Dekalb Airport is having an air show. A very good pilot friend of mine will have four of his planes at the show and has offered any of them to me to use that morning. The air show begins at noon, so we would need to do this early if possible and have the plane back at the airstrip by nine thirty or ten at the latest."

"I need to do it at precisely nine o'clock, so this sounds as if it is all falling into place perfectly."

"I know we don't usually discuss your projects in too many details, but I am just putting two and two together here and I imagine we will be applying the paint from the airplane?"

"That is correct."

"Then I know which plane we will use. The guy who is letting us use the paint applicator e-mailed me the dimensions of the device, and I know which plane it will fit into the best, and how we can release the paint from under the plane."

"Great," Juniper answered. "I am worried about something," Juniper confessed.

"What's that?" Nick asked.

"I have a feeling that I might get arrested from this job as it will be difficult to have a flight plan, do what I have planned, and land a plane that will be seen by probably hundreds of people."

"I have thought about that," Nick answered. "I have a few ideas if you want to hear them."

"Of course."

"I thought of this when I was talking to the guy who is making the paint. He said he has something that we can spray on the outside of the plane twenty or so minutes before takeoff. So, we will take off looking like a normal plane. After exactly thirty minutes, the spray will turn sky blue, making the plane invisible to the human eye. We will have to hope for a sunny day and blue skies. The effect only lasts ten minutes. After ten minutes, the effect wears off and we land, looking once again like a normal plane."

"Brilliant," Juniper said.

"That doesn't make us invisible to radar," Nick stated.

"Oh, right. Darn it."

"But, I have another friend that can lend us a jamming device that will mess up the radar tracking us for the right price."

"You have thought of everything, my friend," Juniper stated.

"I like you to be happy, sir," Nick answered.

"I am very happy."

After Juniper finished his phone call, he saw that Junior and Booger were out in the yard. Junior took one look at Juniper's beaming face and knew he would say yes to anything she asked. When he was in a good mood, he was so easy.

"Booger be real good dog today," she began. "He learn a lot. Bestest and smartestest dog I ever had."

"It's the only dog you have ever had," Juniper answered with a smile.

"Don't make me give him the command to attack you," she said dead seriously.

"What, pray tell, is your wacky secret command to attack?" Juniper asked.

"Big Mac," Junior whispered. Her eyes were extremely serious.

"Big Mac?" Juniper questioned.

"Shhh!" Junior said. She shot him an angry glare. "Do you want Booger to rip you to pieces?"

Juniper tried not to laugh and answered, "No."

"Then don't you dare say that again unless you want to lose an arm or something."

"OK. Can I ask then how you came up with the command in which you use the word meaning the delicious sandwich from McDonald's that has two all beef patties, special sauce, lettuce, cheese, pickles, all on a sesame seed bun?"

"You know how I love that sandwich, right?"

"Yes," Juniper answered.

"Well, sometimes I wake up in the morning or it just hits me sometime in the day and I feel like I am just going to go crazy if I don't have one." Juniper covers Booger's ears. "Big Macs are awesome and sometimes I have a Big Mac attack. So, the command for attack is Big Mac. Get it?" She released her hands from Booger's ears.

"Once again, I must commend you on your creativity."

"Yeah," she says, "you are not the only creative one in this family."

"Don't get mean now," Juniper said. "I thought you were trying to butter me up for something a minute ago and now you have somehow gotten off track."

"Oh yeah," Junior said. "Booger has been such a good boy he deserves a reward."

"What kind of reward would that be? Did you already get him hooked on foot long hot dogs?"

"No, Booger said, although they taste good, delicious, and awesome, he cannot eat another one until the name is changed."

"He said that?" Juniper asked.

"He did."

"Then what kind of reward would he like?"

"I think he has been hinting around about ice cream," Junior said. "I know he has never eated ice cream, but I told him all about it this morning and I told him how it makes your whole face feel like a circus and he wanted to try some."

"Wow," Juniper answered. "Ice cream really makes your whole face feel like a circus?"

"Yep. The big top! Clowns, elephant tricks, trapeze flying people, lion tamers, and all that, just having a big time party in my mouth. I told Booger about it before we started training and he wanted some, so he been real good trying to listen today."

"Well, we better get him some ice cream so he can feel what it's like to have a circus in his mouth."

Junior rode to the ice cream shop with Booger on her lap, talking to him the entire way, discussing what flavor he might like to try. She told him, although chocolate is a delicious taste, dogs and chocolate for some reason don't mix well together. She suggested about twenty-five different flavors and at one point Juniper started to wonder if she had the entire menu memorized. She finally decided in her monologue that Booger should start his ice cream journey like most people do, with vanilla. Vanilla, she said, is only boring once you have discovered all the other wonderful flavors. She told him he was lucky to be able to experience vanilla without any knowledge of the other thousands of flavors out there in the world. So, it was decided, Booger would have a vanilla waffle cone.

"Waffle cones are one of the most awesome things in the whole world," Junior said to Juniper as they pulled into the parking lot of the ice cream shop. "Best thing ever invented," she said.

"Better than television?" Juniper asked.

"Yep," she answered, without hesitation. "I like them almost better than you."

"Oh, wow, thanks," Juniper said with a smile. "I rate just above waffle cones on your list of wonderful things."

"Barely," she answered.

Mr. Teca hosed off some dropped ice cream from under a table before the ants could get it, as Juniper and Junior arrived. When he saw Junior, his face lit up.

"Miss Rio, Miss Rio, Miss Rio," he chanted. "I have a major, super, gigantic surprise for you. I am so, so happy you is here."

Mr. Teca ran inside the building shaped like an ice cream cone as Junior, Juniper, and Booger got settled at one of the outdoor booths. Booger smelled the ground where Mr. Teca had just hosed away spilt ice cream, and his tail started to wag excitedly.

A moment later, Mr. Teca appeared in the doorway with something behind his back and announced to Junior, "Close your eyes, Miss Rio." He walked over to her and from behind his back he revealed a heaping waffle cone of lima bean ice cream that she had desired on her last visit. "Open eyes," he commanded. Mr. Teca chanted with glee, "Lima bean, lima bean, lima bean." His face beamed with pride.

Taking the waffle cone in her hand, Junior asked, "You did this for me?" Mr. Teca nodded. "That is just one of the nicest things anyone has ever done for me in my life." Junior licked the cone and then took a bite. "It's

98

awesome!" she said. "Better than I could have ever dreamed it would be."

"Who is this special guy?" Mr. Teca said, petting Booger's head.

"His name is Booger, and he has been a real good boy today, training to be a good doggy."

"He deserves a reward!" Mr. Teca said.

"That's why we are here," Junior answered. "I was thinking he might like to start his ice cream journey with vanilla. And my brother will probably have his usual boring Mint Oreo."

Juniper nodded as Mr. Teca turned to fetch the ice creams.

"Is that really good?" Juniper asked of the lima bean ice cream Junior was eating.

"It's like a circus *and* a carnival in my mouth," she answered.

Mr. Teca came out and handed Juniper his waffle cone heaping with Mint Oreo ice cream. He put down on the ground a bowl of vanilla ice cream that had obvious chunks of something embedded in it.

"I have a dog of my own," Mr. Teca said. "Just this morning, I buy him some doggy biscuits that I not bring home yet. I blend them with vanilla ice cream for what I call doggy biscuit surprise!"

Booger stuck his nose directly in the ice cream and jumped back with surprise at the cold. Slowly, he sniffed and licked at it again. Before long, he had his face buried in the bowl licking and chomping the ice cream and doggy biscuits.

"He a good dog," Junior said as she watched him eating the ice cream.

"You are a good trainer," Juniper offered.

"I sure am," Junior agreed. "I sure am."

Chapter 20

The luncheon with the Vargas family and Emilio went well. Stuart felt a happiness that he had not felt in quite some time. The food Mrs. Vargas made was better than any Mexican restaurant fare that Stuart had ever eaten. Emilio brought a guitar and could play as well as promised. Stuart and Emilio had made plans to get together and play again. Stuart wondered if he should show him his secret studio atop the King Cone building. He finally decided he would wait and see how the friendship evolved before sharing his biggest secret.

Revived after his day off, Stuart arrived at work earlier than usual. Before entering the building, he looked up to admire the six story replica of the soft serve ice cream sitting atop the golden cone. It amazed him every time he laid eyes on it and he felt overwhelmed with pride to be the owner of Atlanta's tallest building.

Stuart's assistant sat at his desk, busily typing while reading from a paper he had sitting beside the keyboard. He did not hear or see Stuart enter his office space.

"Good morning, Ken," Stuart announced.

Ken was not only startled to see Stuart standing in front of him, but he also found it odd that Stuart remembered his name correctly. He took that as a good sign that Stuart was back on his game.

"Good morning, sir," he said.

"Try that again," Stuart said.

"Good morning, Stuart," he said with a smile.

"That's better. I would like to nail down the plans today for the grand opening ceremonies for the building."

"OK," Ken answered. "What time would you like me to set the meeting?"

"Noon," Stuart said. "Please let the staff know that lunch will be provided and I apologize for the short notice. If the staff brought their lunch they can leave it in one of the fridges here for tomorrow."

"Very good," Ken said jotting down some notes. "I will email everybody immediately. From where would you like me to order lunch?"

"If you will take care of the email, I will take care of ordering lunch," Stuart said.

As soon as Stuart sat down at his desk, he had the yellow pages out looking for the phone number for Hog's. He didn't know if Mr. Henry catered, but decided he would give him a call. The phone rang twice before Mr. Henry picked up.

"Is this Mr. Henry?" Stuart asked.

"You got him," Mr. Henry answered.

"I met you the other night and told you my name was Billy Green. I don't know if you remember me or not."

"Of course I remember you. I remember that didn't sound like your real name."

"You are right, it isn't. My real name is Stuart King."

"The King Cone, Stuart King?"

"Yes sir, that is me."

"Well I'll be. What can I do for you, Mr. King?"

"Please call me Stuart. I was wondering if you do any catering. I have a lunch meeting with about fifteen people today at noon and when I was thinking about what I wanted to eat, your burgers popped into my mind. I know it's real short notice."

"I do some catering on occasion when my brother is around to help. Just so happens he is here today and the city is redoing the sidewalk in front of the restaurant and causing such a commotion and making such a blasted mess, I don't expect a big lunch crowd today."

"That's wonderful," Stuart said.

"What can I bring y'all?"

"Burgers, fries, some of those delicious onion rings," Stuart paused to think. "Did you have barbeque on the menu?" he asked.

"Yep, I have sliced pork and a beef brisket that is to die for. Y'all might also like my chicken wings. Best in the city, I guarantee that!"

"You know what," Stuart said, "you just make up the menu yourself. I know I said fifteen people, but pretend we have twice that. I want enough food for people to take home, and I want them to experience all your wonderful creations."

Mr. Henry chuckled on the other end of the phone. "How about dessert? My brother makes the world's best key lime pie. He also makes a cinnamon roll cake that you will be thinking about for days."

"Bring it on. I can barely wait. If you will call when you leave the restaurant, I will have somebody meet you at the loading dock at the back of the building, and we have an elevator there that will bring you straight up to me."

"See you at about a quarter to twelve."

"Thank you, Mr. Henry. Thank you so much."

"You are welcome, Stuart. Thank you for your business."

Stuart stayed busy all morning making plans for the meeting and the grand opening ceremony he was going to pitch at the lunch conference. He had given Mr. Henry his personal cell number and it rang at eleven thirty.

"Hello," he answered.

"I'm leaving the store now," Mr. Henry said. "Should be at your back dock in about ten or so minutes depending on traffic."

"I'll be down there waiting for you," Stuart answered.

Ten minutes later, Mr. Henry backed up to the dock in a white van. Stuart and Ken were waiting with carts to help carry the food upstairs. When Mr. Henry got out of the van, he shook hands with Stuart and Stuart introduced Ken, getting his name right once again.

102

The food was all held in silver containers that were too hot to touch with bare hands. Mr. Henry handed Stuart and Ken oven gloves, and they quickly transferred the food to the carts. On the elevator to the top of the building where the meeting would be held, the smells from the food filled the small area and Stuart felt as if he might start drooling. Mr. Henry noticed him breathing deeply through his nose and he laughed out loud.

"You smelling those chicken wings," Mr. Henry said. "My friend Mash gets them every chance he can. Some folks who moved out of the city come back religiously every week, just so they can get an order or two of wings."

"If they are half as good as the burger I had, we are in for a real treat."

"They so good they gonna make that burger taste like an old worn out shoe."

"Should I try one now?" Stuart asked, with his eyes popping open at Mr. Henry like a school boy.

"Go on," Mr. Henry said. Mr. Henry knew the container the wings were in, and he propped open the top so Stuart could grab a wing. After Stuart grabbed one, Mr. Henry instructed Ken to get one as well. Mr. Henry watched with amusement as they bit into the wings. They bit in unison and in unison their knees went weak.

"Oh my goodness gracious!" Stuart said

"Good giggly wiggly!" Ken pronounced.

Mr. Henry just laughed. "Told you."

They set the silver containers on tables Ken had set up and they placed the plates, silverware, cups, and iced tea along the serving line.

"I gotta get on back to the restaurant in case we get an unexpected lunch rush," Mr. Henry said. "I will come pick up the silver and bring the bill this afternoon."

"That won't be necessary," Stuart answered. "I will bring it back to you this evening on my way home. I drove my truck into work today and those silver containers will all sit safely in the back. I think I might need some wings for dinner!" he finished with a huge smile.

"All righty then," Mr. Henry said. "See you then."

The lunch was an incredible hit. The staff could not decide what tasted best as they tried and tried until everyone was stuffed. With filled bellies and smiling faces all around the room, the staff members were called for the meeting by Stuart.

"I am sorry I sprung this meeting on all of you. I hope those of you who packed a lunch today will forgive me." The room laughed. "I would like to finalize the plans today for the grand opening celebration we planned earlier in the year, which was put on hold because of all the snow we had back in February. I have studied the calendar this morning and have chosen Saturday, March 22 to hold the ceremony. Does anyone foresee a problem with this date?" The group studied their calendars and nobody found any problems with the proposed date. "There are a lot of events planned in the city and the surrounding cities on this date and hopefully it will help us pull in more people to join us. There is a music festival that starts at noon in Centennial Park. Stone Mountain is having a chili cook-off. The Peachtree Dekalb Airport is having an air show. And the Atlanta Aquarium is unveiling a new dolphin show. I was thinking if we had the grand opening ceremony at nine o'clock, we might get some of the people planning to attend the other events if we offer free breakfast and free ice cream, of course."

"Does Mr. Henry's restaurant cook breakfast?" Ken asked.

"His restaurant sure does," Stuart answered.

"Maybe we could get him to cater the breakfast at the grand opening," Ken offered.

"That's a great idea!" Stuart answered. Everyone nodded their heads in agreement. "I will ask him about that, this evening, when I return his food containers. I was also thinking that we might play up the whole spring idea and rebirth and give away plants or something like that," Stuart said, hesitantly. "Does anybody have any contacts with Home Depot or Lowes or anywhere we might get some help on plants to give away?"

"I have a contact at Pike's Nursery," a lady named Susan answered. "Have you ever heard the Walter Reeve's Garden Show on Saturday morning?" she asked.

"I have," Stuart answered. "I really like that show. He sounds like a great guy."

"I can try to get him to broadcast the show from here on that morning," Susan said.

"Great idea, Susan," Stuart said. "Get on that and let me know what they say."

The meeting ended with everyone packing Styrofoam containers with the leftovers and although they were full, they all tried to eat either one more piece of the key lime pie or the cinnamon roll cake. Both desserts were beyond fabulous.

Stuart drove his truck around to the back of Hog's. He knocked on the door and Mr. Henry opened it with a smile. As he unloaded the silver containers, Mr. Henry noticed they had been cleaned.

"You didn't have to clean them," Mr. Henry said.

"I know," Stuart answered. "I was trying to show my appreciation for helping me on such short notice."

"You cleaned these yourself?" Mr. Henry asked.

"Yes," Stuart answered.

"Let me get this right," Mr. Henry said. "You are the CEO of King Cone and are probably worth about one hundred million dollars and you didn't ask one of your thousands of employees to wash this for you?"

"Nope."

"Amazing," Mr. Henry said. "I like that."

"I have a philosophy about my job that I try to remember every day," Stuart said. "I don't ask any of my employees to do anything that I would not do myself."

"You must be a good man to work for," Mr. Henry said with a gentle smile.

"I hope so," Stuart said. "Now, how about I settle up for today's lunch."

Mr. Henry produced a bill from his pocket and Stuart paid, leaving a very, very generous tip. He also left a fifty dollar tip for Mr. Henry's brother who had made the cinnamon roll cake.

Once the bill was settled and Stuart had convinced Mr. Henry that his tip was not too much, he asked him about catering the breakfast for the grand opening.

"March 22, you say?" Mr. Henry asked.

"March 22," Stuart answered. "That is correct."

"I think that is the day my friend Mash is going to his air show," Mr. Henry said.

"Peachtree Dekalb Airport is having an air show on that day," Stuart confirmed.

Mr. Henry looked at his calendar and said, "I don't see a problem with that date. My biscuits are the best around."

"I bet they are," Stuart said. "I can't wait to try one."

"March 22 is going to be a big day!" Mr. Henry said.

"It's going to be the best day ever!" Stuart answered. "The best day ever!"

Chapter 21

Junior had another nightmare and she screamed. Juniper raced down the hall. He arrived at her bedside just as she sat up filled with fear. She flipped her left leg over the side of the bed, ready to flee.

"I'm here," Juniper said, as he grabbed her arm firmly to let her know he was there. "You are asleep. Junior, it's Juniper. You are asleep. Wake up."

Junior suddenly awoke and her eyes shot open. "I can't go," she said.

"OK," Juniper answered, having no idea what she was talking about.

"I can't go. I want to go, but I just can't go. I'm sorry."

Juniper didn't say anything as he was not even sure what to think.

Junior lightly slapped Juniper's face. "I'm not asleep," she said. "Can't go, can't go."

"You can't go where?" Juniper asked.

"On your new art project," Junior answered. "I'm being so, so sorry. I'm being so sorry, Juniper," she said, with tears in her eyes.

"That's OK," Juniper said, relieved. "Someone probably needs to stay on the ground and take care of Booger."

"Booger needs me and something bad going to happen in the plane. I saw it."

"What did you see?" Juniper asked.

"Lightning went through the plane," she said. "Or maybe it was 'lectricity. But it was totally bright and really yellow and white and loud and then people were lying all over the floor. You were one of them. Somebody stood over you with a sword or light saber or something that held the 'lectricity."

"It was just a dream," Juniper assured her.

"You going to find out it's more than a dream."

"OK, OK," Juniper said. He did not want to talk her back into going, as he was glad she was not, just in case something strange *did* happen. Although she did not know it, he had set up papers and a will with his lawyer that would have her well taken care of. He did not want to think of this, and he put the idea out of his mind.

Junior fell back to sleep while Juniper scratched her back. Once back in his own bed, it took Juniper about half an hour to clear his mind and fall back to sleep. He worried for a while that her dream actually meant something. Juniper made a mental list of all that could go wrong, and Juniper tried to imagine how long he might be in jail if caught, and what it would be like to live in a tiny cell.

Juniper and Junior awoke to rain. It pounded against the house and windows like the big bad wolf wanting to come in. At one point, Junior jumped up and yelled, "Not by the hair on my chinny chin chin!" Juniper looked up from his coffee cup and online news to give her a funny look.

"I was hoping to work in the studio after I finish this cup of coffee. Are you going to be alright in here?"

"Yes," she answered. "Booger will protect me." She stated this with such seriousness and sincere belief that Juniper once again had to pause what he was doing to stare at her with disbelief. Booger was not even one foot tall. He probably weighed four or five pounds soaking wet, and if he bit you, it might hurt a tiny amount. You might need a small band aid. If Juniper had known a dog would have this effect on Junior, he would have bought her one years ago.

"OK," Juniper said finishing his cup of coffee, "if you need me, you know where I will be. You can either use an umbrella and come over, or you can call me on my cell."

"We won't need you," Junior answered.

"What are you two going to do?" Juniper asked.

"Booger wants to build a fort and watch Animal Planet."

"Sounds like a plan," Juniper said. "I'll be back for lunch. Maybe we could order pizza or something."

"Can I pick the toppings?" she asked.

"Sure. We will get two pizzas. You pick yours and I will pick mine."

Junior could somehow take a normal list of toppings and turn a pizza into a nightmare for the normal eater. The last time they ordered pizza, she ordered without Juniper knowing—triple pineapple, double bacon, triple onion, no cheese, extra marinara sauce, quadruple pepperoni, and triple black olive. Not only was the concoction absolutely disgusting, it cost almost forty dollars for one pizza!

Inside the studio, Juniper sat in his chair and pulled the lever that allowed his feet to stick out. He took a few deep breaths and got his mind right. He told himself, *This is a project I want to do. This art project is important. I am going to go through with it and do this project and it is all going to be OK.* He was always very nervous in the weeks before a project took place. Juniper worried about every little detail and obsessed about what could go wrong. It was probably one of the reasons he never got caught—that, and good luck.

Juniper knew he needed art and creative work to keep his mind clear. He looked around the studio and tried to decide on what he would like to work. He had a few different projects, already in the works, he could finish or advance. His ceramic Dr. Seuss building was dried, and had been bisque fired if he wanted to glaze it. He didn't. He had been working on a sculpture in wood of a dancing Native American. That project took a lot of concentration which he did not think he had at this moment. He needed something fun and playful.

Juniper's eyes lit up as he remembered the bag of stuff he had collected at the tractor repair shop. A week earlier, the tractor he used to bush hog the pasture had broken down, and he had taken the part he suspected to be the culprit of the breakdown over to the tractor shop in town. Juniper had a habit of looking in trash cans, trash piles, dumpsters, and other places where people discarded their unwanted items. The tractor shop had an old metal barrel in which people threw away their trash. Next to the barrel, sat items too heavy to go in the barrel, such as odd pieces of metal, which people thought were unrecyclable and fit for the junkyard.

Juniper's eyes first found the gloves, sitting atop the overfilled barrel. They were not your run of the mill, normal gloves. These were gloves that went all the way up to a big man's shoulders. He wondered what they had been used for. Next to the barrel, on the floor, sat a pile of bolts of the like Juniper or most people have never seen. The bolts were almost as big as bagels or donuts—a little smaller, but almost that size. They were coated with a small layer of rust that Juniper found beautiful. Orange flakes mixed with grays, flashes of silver and a wide array of burnt oranges. He had to have them.

"What are you all going to do with these gloves and these bolts?" Juniper asked, pointing at the trash barrel and the pile of bolts next to it.

"Throwing them away," the store owner answered.

"Can I take them off your hands?" Juniper asked.

"Sure," the owner answered. "You gonna make some art out of that?"

"I just might," Juniper answered, not sure whether the man was making fun of him or not. He took the stuff anyway.

Breaking from the memory, Juniper jumped out of the recliner, and found, next to the door, the two boxes in which he had carried the goods home. He pulled out the gloves. He found a tape measure and found them to be twenty inches long. Juniper then scoured the studio for

110

something at least twenty inches long to glue them to. The only thing he could find was a heavy metal shelf intended for a warehouse. He thought it would be perfect as it measured twenty-two inches. Juniper put the shelf flat upon the ground in the area of the studio he wished to work in and turned on some tunes.

With Todd Snider pouring out of the studio speakers, Juniper's thoughts turned from music to adhesives. He had a collection of caulk, glue, and this and that. He chose a tube of something called Liquid Nails and popped the tube into a caulking gun. Juniper flipped over the gloves and generously coated the backs of the gloves with the Liquid Nails. He then visualized where on the metal shelf he would place the gloves, and then he added more Liquid Nails to the shelf. Satisfied he had enough adhesive to hold the gloves, he placed the gloves on the glue and pressed them down. Little did he know or care, Juniper had applied enough glue to hold a lawn mower.

With the leftover glue, Juniper glued the almost donut or bagel size bolts around the perimeter of the shelf. He had enough bolts to go all the way around and he had six leftover. He sat those on the shelf next to his radio, with thoughts of what he might do with them. Standing away from the piece, he studied it and decided it was not right. The rusted bolts looked awesome but the gloves did not. He visualized them as different colors and finally decided an antique white would be perfect.

Juniper sauntered over to a wooden shelf where he kept cans of spray paint. He probably had at least seventy-five cans or more. It seemed as though he had acquired the habit of picking up a can or two of spray paint every time he visited a home improvement store, just in case he might need it at some point in the future. Shuffling through his inventory, he pumped his fist with delight, discovering a brand new can of antique white.

Juniper shook the can vigorously as he stood over his target. Sticking a cinderblock and an old boot under the top of the artwork allowed Juniper a better angle to

111

paint. He mashed the button atop the spray paint can and watched as the lengthy gloves turned from a greasy black to antique white. Twice, Juniper paused in his painting to shake the can. He sprayed every last bit of paint, even the last drops which sputtered from the can, plopping drops above the smooth layer of antique white. The can sputtered and he thought, *Texture is grand. Texture is beautiful.* The can finally blew air and the antique white was gone.

Juniper's cell rang and he realized that it was past noon. "Hello," he answered.

"I ordered pizza," Junior said on the other end of the line.

"Did you order two?" Juniper asked, worried.

"Yes," she answered. "I got you something boring like you like and me something totally the bomb delicious."

"OK," Juniper said. "I will be there in just a minute. My piece needs some time to dry, anyway."

"Do you have a fifty dollar bill anywhere in the house I can give the driver?"

"Fifty dollars for two pizzas?"

"Yeah," Junior answered. "Can you believe your boring pizza cost eight dollars?"

"Ummm..." Juniper mumbled doing math in his head, "that means, with tip, your pizza cost thirty eight or so dollars?"

"Oh, no," she answered, with surprise in her voice. "I was forgetting the tip. My pizza is going to cost forty-two dollars."

"Forty two dollars for a pizza!"

"Hey!" Junior yelled through the phone. "Good taste ain't cheap! I am sorry you have such simple and boring taste."

Juniper was not mad about the money. They had plenty of money. He just could not believe that a delivery pizza could cost forty two dollars.

"Look in the kitchen junk drawer. I remember seeing three twenty dollar bills in there the other day. Just give the driver the sixty bucks and tell him to keep the change."

"Do you want to know what I got on my pizza?" Junior asked.

"No! I don't think I even want to smell it or even see it from a distance. The pizza man is probably going to need help carrying it in!" he joked.

Ignoring his request not to know, she began, "It is a deep dish pizza with triple banana pepper, quadruple green olive, double mushroom, double jalapeño..."

Juniper hung up his cell phone, as he felt he might throw up all over the artwork he had worked on so hard all morning.

Part VI

Chapter 22

The next few weeks leading up to the air show fly by, no pun intended. Life at home is fairly calm, and Mr. Henry needs me to work a few times here and there at the restaurant, which enables me to save up a little cash for my outing. Somewhere along the line, I decide I am so nervous about missing the beginning of the air show that I am going to get there the night before. I will either stay up all night or I will find a place to catch a few hours of sleep. I know it is risky, but this air show is everything to me. If I tell Mama I am spending the night out with Charles, she won't remember that it is the night before the air show. Grandma might remember and be suspicious. I will deal with that when the time comes.

Every night before I go to bed, I study the directions Judd gave me. By the fourth night I have them memorized, but I study them every night nonetheless. I am so excited, I can barely function and everyone in my life, besides Mama, notices the change in me. Since Ms. Monique sees me every week day, she notices the most and on Friday she asks to see me after class.

"Mash," she begins, bobbing her tea bag, thrice used, up and down in her cup. "Do you think about anything other than airplanes?" There she goes with the questions. I love her probably more than my own mother, but my goodness she asks a lot of questions.

"I do, Ms. Monique," I answer. "The air show is coming soon and I am a little preoccupied," I say.

"When exactly is the air show?" she asks.

"Tomorrow," I say sheepishly.

"Tomorrow!" she gasps. "Tomorrow! You are supposed to take my cell phone with you," she says.

"I know," I say. "I was going to ask you after school."

"No you weren't," she says, still trying to catch her breath.

"I was," I say. "I really was."

Ms. Monique is so nervous and out of sorts that she pulls a *brand* new tea bag out of her desk drawer and adds it to the already steaming cup of water and thrice used bag. She dips it in and out of the water with a motion that reminds me of a fisherman. Ms. Monique's bobbing of the bag is hypnotic and I fall into her trap.

"Are you putting yourself in danger," she asks. Always the questions.

My eyes fix on the bobbing tea bag and I answer, "Not really."

"What do you mean?" Ms. Monique asks.

I reluctantly tell her my plan.

"That is not a plan at all!" she answers. "In this crazy plan of yours, you should at least have some crazy part where you sneak inside one of the airplanes and find a little place to snuggle in for the night to get some sleep. Don't just sit out in the open all night where someone might see you and harm you."

"Great idea!" I say. I hold out my hand for the cell phone and she puts it in my palm.

"Be safe," she says, sincerely. "Be safe, Mash."

Ever since the day Father Phillip gave me the Saint Christopher medal, I have been carrying it around with me. After I leave school, I finger the medal in my pocket and decide to pay him a visit. As I walk into the sanctuary, he walks out of one of the confession booths and spots me.

"Are you here to make a confession?" he asks. He loves this joke.

"I might need to next week," I say deadpan. Father Phillip breaks into one of his monster laughs in which I think he might end up on the floor, rolling around in a fit. When he settles down, I ask, "What is it like outside of the city?"

Father Phillip thinks for a moment, his eyes look up into his head and he cups his chin with his left hand.

116

"It is quieter, slower, calmer. On my rare trips out of the city, I have seen strangers talking to other strangers."

"I talk to strangers all the time," I say.

"Yeah, but you are different," he says.

"What else?"

"There is just a different feel."

"Better?" I ask.

"I don't think so," Father Phillip answers. "I have had many opportunities to transfer to churches away from the city, but I have always wanted to stay here."

"Why?" I ask.

"Well, there is just something that grabs you about a city. I know the city can be loud, hectic, some elements are scary, some of it is smelly, and it seems as if there are some parts of it that never sleep or give you a break from all of its moving parts. But that is what I love about the city—it is alive! There is life in a city. It can be vibrant, fresh, and exciting. I love to hear the Georgia Tech band playing at halftime and practicing in the early evenings of fall. I can hear the crowds screaming their lungs out from the front steps of the church or sitting at my desk when I have my window propped open. I can see the fireworks shooting over at Turner Field after every Friday night home game the Braves play. Even the sirens of the police cars, fire trucks, and ambulances give me some strange comfort to know there are people at the ready to help other people. I love seeing the tourists wandering around, trying to find the Georgia Aquarium and the Coca-Cola Museum. I like how I can walk two blocks and see all different races pass me by. A city is humanity in a bottle— all the good and all the bad and everything in between."

"I never thought of it all like that," I say. "There are certain parts of the city I like. I do enjoy seeing all the crazy football fans. On college football Saturdays, the city just seems like it is buzzing. I usually just walk over by the Varsity and watch all the people in their gold and the visiting teams in their orange or baby blue or red. Sometimes, I just want to hear nothing, though."

"Sometimes, nothing can be the loudest sound there is," Father Phillip says.

I have no idea what that means and I don't have time to ask him to explain further, as one of his flock, as he calls them, comes in for a chat. I feel as though I should share him so he can shepherd the newcomer and I thank him for his time.

Before turning his attention away from me, he says, "Mash, be careful this weekend. Bring Saint Christopher with you and I will say prayers for you."

Without saying a word, I pull Saint Christopher out of my pocket and hold it up for him to see. He smiles at me like I imagine my own father would if he was still alive.

Back at home, I see Mama asleep on the couch and smell a sweet scent surrounding her. So, I don't even have to lie to her about where I will be. She will not wake up until the morning and she usually doesn't know what day of the week it is, so she will just think I am at school if she thinks about me at all. Grandma's door is shut. She isn't asleep, I know. Mama was probably acting a fool and Grandma just went into her room and closed off the world and is lost in a book. I think about just leaving without telling her my lie, but I don't want her to worry.

I pack my bag and rehearse in my mind the lie I will tell her. I hate lying and because I feel so guilty when I do it, I am a terrible liar. I beat myself up inside my head about it while I pack my backpack with a few things. When I am finished packing and ready to go, I take a deep breath and decide not to lie. I decide not to tell the whole truth either.

I knock lightly on Grandma's bedroom door. She tells me to come on in and I crack the door so she hopefully won't see the backpack slung across my shoulder. I think I should have left it in the living room or kitchen, but it is too late for that now.

"I'm going out, Grandma," I say.

"OK, baby."

"I'll be back tomorrow," I say, "so don't worry about me tonight when you don't hear me come in." I didn't lie.

"You staying the night with Charles?" she asks.

"No, ma'am." I haven't lied yet.

"You staying with one of your other friends?"

She got me now. "No ma'am."

"You heading to the air show early?"

I open the door all the way. "Yes ma'am."

"Um huh. Thanks for not lying to me, Mash. You never were any good at it anyway," she laughs. "Can I somehow talk you out of going?"

"I'm afraid not," I say.

"Come on in and sit on the bed then," she says. "I won't fuss or fight you if you will just take with you something I have here in my drawer."

"OK."

She slowly gets out of her rocking chair and puts her book down. She pulls open the bottom drawer and pushes some clothes to the side. I wonder in that instant why people always put their secret stuff in the bottom drawer. She pulls out something that looks like a plastic gun and sits back down in her rocking chair.

"This," she says, "was supposed to be a police issue taser gun, but the State ultimately decided that it was too powerful and it was supposed to be destroyed."

A little shocked that Grandma has a taser gun that was thought to be too powerful for police use, I ask the obvious question, "How did you happen to end up with one?"

"Promise not to tell?" she asks.

"I promise."

"The head librarian's husband was on the committee that tested them. He was also responsible for destroying them. He did destroy most of them. He just forgot a few." Grandma cracks a sly smile. "She knew I lived with my daughter and two grandsons in a pretty rough part of town and she gave me one. She taught me how to use it and you will have to listen to me tell you how to use it. Then you can put it in your backpack and I will try my best not to worry about you."

"Sounds like a deal," I say.

She shows me how it works and I tuck it away in the bottom of my backpack. I kiss her on her cheek and she grabs my neck and squeezes me in a way that only grandmothers can. She plants a big juicy kiss on my cheek and we tell each other we love one another. As I am about to shut her door and leave, she stops me.

"Feels good not to lie, doesn't it?"

"Yes ma'am. It feels really good."

I leave the house for my first journey out of the city, with a great feeling in my belly and a super powerful taser gun in my backpack.

Chapter 23

Stuart looked at the clock in his office and realized it was ten minutes after five. He put down his pen and shut down his computer. Since he met Emilio, he had found a balance between work and music. Stuart had always been such a go-getter that his laser like focus sometimes had the ability to throw other parts of his life off course and out of balance. When he discovered music, he forgot about work. When he was fueled by the passion of work, he had forgotten about a personal life and his hobbies. Emilio had changed all of that and taught him that it *was* possible to have both; that it *was* important to have both.

Once inside his car, he dialed Emilio on his cell phone.

"Are we still rehearsing tonight?" he asked Emilio when he answered.

"Of course," Emilio answered. "We have a gig tomorrow! I am going to be a little later than I thought. My niece, Cynthia, needs me to come by her house to help her with a school project. She is studying methods of transportation and needs to interview a truck driver. Family first—right?"

"Right on," Stuart answered. "Take your time and I will see you when you get here."

The grand opening ceremony for the King Cone building was the following morning and Stuart and Emilio's band was scheduled to play the event. This would be their first time playing in front of a crowd. They had played for Mr. and Mrs. Vargas and Cynthia and Oscar, but never for people they did not know. Stuart was overjoyed with the thought of his first show.

At home, he looked in the fridge to find a plate of food Mrs. Vargas had made and left for him to heat up and eat. She had stuck a little note on it with heating instructions and wishes for good luck the following morning at the gig. Stuart had fallen in love with Mr. and

Mrs. Vargas and truly thought of them as family. They were so good to him, and he, in turn, was extra good to them.

As he punched the buttons of the microwave, he asked the voice recognition system to turn the television to the Weather Channel. After heating up the plate, Stuart sat down at the kitchen table to eat and watch the weather. His phone rang after a few bites. It was Mr. Henry.

"My favorite cook," Stuart said answering with joy.

"How are you buddy?" Mr. Henry asked.

"I am doing well," Stuart answered.

"You've come a long way since that first night I met you in the restaurant," Mr. Henry commented. "You seem very happy."

"I am, Mr. Henry," Stuart said. "I am."

"I am so happy for you." Mr. Henry paused. "Now," he continued, "let's get down to the business at hand. We are all set to go for tomorrow morning. I touched base with all my help a few minutes ago and they know what to do and what is expected of them. I was hoping you would be able to meet a friend of mine named Mash tomorrow, but I can't get in touch with him."

"Did you try his cell?" Stuart asked.

Mr. Henry's laugh almost came through the phone.

"He doesn't have a cell phone," Mr. Henry stated. "He doesn't even have a home phone."

"Are you serious?" Stuart said. "I'll get him one," Stuart offered.

"I know you could and I could too. I've thought about it many, many times, but we can't save the world. There are a whole lot more important things in the world besides telephones. My friend Mash is going to be OK without one. I just wish you would have the chance to meet him. He is a special kid."

"How about you tell him I want to meet him one day and I will buy him lunch. Would that be fine?"

"I usually make him work for it when I feed him, but I think one time will be alright."

"Sounds good," Stuart said, intrigued by the kid Mr. Henry complimented.

"Now," Mr. Henry said, bringing the conversation back to the matter at hand. "Is there anything new I need to know before I see you bright and early tomorrow morning?"

"I can't think of a thing," Stuart answered. "I was just watching the weather and it is going to be a perfect Spring day. Seventy four degrees, blue skies without a cloud anywhere near the state of Georgia. So the weather man says, anyway!"

"I believe it and you deserve it. If there is nothing else, I will see you in the morning."

"I can't wait."

The two hung up their phones and Stuart quickly finished his plate of food. Knowing Emilio would not be there for at least another hour, he sprinted to his bedroom, stripped, and put on his bathing suit. His mom always said not to swim for at least an hour after eating, but he never understood the rule and had always disregarded it without consequences. Some kid, Stuart decided, must have eaten a huge meal and had a cramp and died in a freak accident. Maybe the kid didn't even know how to swim very well! Stuart decided that this one kid's mistake had made kids all over the world suffer and have to wait sixty long minutes after eating because he could not make it back to the side of the pool. Where was his mother anyway? Shouldn't she have been watching him? Shouldn't she be the one to blame? Maybe instead of kids not being able to swim an hour after eating, the rule should be that mothers are not allowed to talk for an hour after kids eat and they have to pay attention to their children.

Because of insurance and lawsuits, there were not many diving boards left in the United States. Stuart's pool had a low board *and* a high board. The pool was twelve feet at its deepest and there was no way somebody was going to hit their face on the bottom of his pool. Divers might twirl around and hit the board or somehow land outside the pool, but Stuart did not worry about these types of things.

Stuart did a one-and-a-half from the low board and entered the water like an Olympian; there was little to no splash. Surfacing from under the water, he looked to the sky, hoping the weather report he had seen was correct. He witnessed a few trace clouds heading east and did not see any more to the west. A bird landed on the board he had just been on and he studied the creature. The bird looked to its left and to its right, pecked at its belly, and looked around again. A passage he had once read about how carefree birds are and how they do not worry about where their next meal is coming from came to mind. Stuart knew he would never need to worry about his next meal, but he thought in this moment, that he would continue to strive to be as carefree as a bird.

Stuart did not realize how long he had been in the pool until he heard the low guttural sounds of Emilio's motorcycle approaching. Stuart looked at his hands and the pruned appearance spoke volumes about how long he had been in the water. Stuart quickly swam to the side and pulled himself out of the pool. Stuart reached inside a sheltered cabinet Mr. Vargas had built, and he pulled out a clean towel and began drying off his face. He inhaled with the towel against his face and the smell of the freshly laundered towel sent his mind spinning. It reminded him of his mother. As he inhaled again, he could see her pinning sheets to a line in their backyard. She had been a wonderful mother.

Stuart met Emilio at the front door and invited him inside. Stuart told him to make himself at home while he quickly changed. Emilio headed down to the basement to set up the equipment, while Stuart took the stairs to the upper level two at a time.

Stuart had written a dozen songs, but had polished six of them to neat and tight little jams. He and Emilio warmed up with Stuart switching from the strumming of chords to finger picking, and back to chords. No matter what Stuart played, Emilio could play along. Stuart was constantly amazed by him. Feeling warmed up and with his juices flowing, he told Emilio that they should run through the six songs and pretend they were live in front of the crowd. No stopping for mess ups, no do overs.

"Don't stop for anything," Emilio told Stuart. "If a giraffe runs across the stage—don't stop."

"I don't think we have wild giraffes in downtown Atlanta," Stuart teased.

"One could escape from the zoo, dude," Emilio countered. "I'm just trying to make a point. No matter how bad you or I might mess up, when you are playing in front of a crowd, you act like nothing happened, forget it, and move on."

"I got it," Stuart assured. "I will not stop playing during a song for any reason."

"Promise?" Emilio asked.

"Promise," Stuart said. "And you?"

"I promise, too."

They practiced beautifully. Emilio smiled at Stuart's passion and the way his songs made him feel. Neither of them had any idea that what they had just promised would have them playing through something almost unimaginable.

The Air Show
&
The King Cone Grand Opening

Mash boarded the MARTA train at six thirty in the evening and took the line heading to the Chamblee station. He had memorized all of this, but looked at his instructions from Judd, just in case. He decided, if he acted like he was supposed to be alone and did not make eye contact with anyone, that he would be fine. He was used to being alone all the time in the city and people never asked him where his parents were. He did not know if it was like this outside of the city, though. Mash had concocted a story, just in case someone asked about his business.

Mash easily found an empty seat, as the train was fairly empty and he slid against the window. The city slowly slipped away. With each stop that took him farther away, his heart beat faster and faster. When the rail lines took the train parallel to the highway, he watched the people in their cars heading away from the city. He thought they would all be happy to be leaving the city, but they just looked like normal people having normal, boring thoughts. Mash thought of what Father Phillip had said about life outside of the city. Maybe it was just incredibly boring. As soon as he thought this, a car full of people laughing hysterically pulled next to the track and slowly pulled past the train. Mash, at one point, was concerned that the driver was laughing so hard that he would not be able to properly drive the car. This was the way he imagined all the people heading out of the city would be— filled with joy and overflowing with happiness. The next car had a man yelling into a cell phone, and the one behind it had a woman who looked like she had had the worst day of her life. The car behind it had something Mash had never seen and something that just blew his mind. The back of the car told him it was a Suburban. It was black and had two kids in the back. Hanging from the ceiling in front of each child was a tiny television playing Sponge Bob Square Pants. Both children were not looking at the screens and angrily looking at the floor. Mash's face fell with disbelief. He saw in the front seat a mom and a dad. They were both dressed in the coolest clothes a kid could have. They had an awesome car with a television, and they weren't happy. *What is the world coming to*, Mash thought.

Before he knew it, the voice over the loud speakers announced the train was pulling into the Chamblee Station. Mash slid out of his seat, and exited the train like he knew where he was going. Judd had written down what bus to take to the Peachtree Dekalb Airport, but Mash did not want to get on a bus. For some reason he felt like someone might talk to him on a bus. Judd told him that the airport was less than a mile from the train station and Mash instantly came up with a plan to find the airport, without asking someone and without getting on the bus.

Mash spotted the bus and line number Judd told him to take and walked to the road where the bus would have to exit the station. Mash sat on a bench and acted like he was waiting on someone. He kept his eye on the bus. When the bus he had been watching pulled out of the station, he followed the direction it travelled and kept his eyes glued to it until it was out of sight, in case it turned. Mash followed the path the bus had taken.

As Mash walked, he thought he might have to stop at some point to wait for another bus to go by and lead the way. Then, he heard the buzz of an airplane coming in for a landing and he thought, *duh, just follow the planes taking off and landing*. He did. They were all small planes, as Peachtree Dekalb Airport was basically a small airport compared to Atlanta's Hartsfield/Jackson Airport, which is one of the world's busiest airports.

Less than fifteen minutes later, the airport came into sight surrounded by a black, metal fence. Mash continued to walk, trying to decide if he could scale the fence or not. He decided he could. As he continued to walk he saw an open drive that led directly into the heart of the airport. Mash looked for a guard house or a security

128

officer, and when he did not see one, he slowly began to walk down the drive and into the airport.

It was a bit past seven thirty, and the sun was settling behind the horizon. The sky filled with beautiful pinks and marvelous oranges and tints of purple Mash had never seen before. He wondered if the sunsets were more beautiful outside of the city or if it was just his heightened state of awareness.

Out of nowhere, a man appeared and asked, "You looking for your dad, bud?"

Mash was quick on his feet and said, "I am meeting him right over there." Mash pointed.

"Were you supposed to meet him by the playground?" the man asked.

A playground at an airport? Mash thought. *Is this a trick question to catch me in a lie?* Mash decided to take a chance and said, "Yes sir, I was supposed to meet him by the playground, but somehow I must have gotten turned around."

"No problem, bud," the man said, putting an arm around his shoulder and leading him around a building. "Beautiful sunset isn't it?"

"Best one I've ever seen," Mash answered, hoping not to give himself away. "There it is," the man said.

Sure enough, there was a playground, in sight of the runway.

"Thank you," Mash said. The sight of the runway almost took his breath away. The man noticed his sudden change in character.

"Would you like me to stay with you until your dad gets here?" the man asked.

"Oh, no," Mash said, recovering nicely. "I just thought I was lost and now I am fine."

"OK, bud," the man said. "Have a great night and enjoy that sunset."

"I will," Mash answered.

As soon as the man rounded the corner and walked out of sight, Mash turned to the runway. He could not believe he was this close to a runway. Before he could even finish his thought, he heard a gentle roar in the sky and turned his eyes to the approaching aircraft. It looked as though it was headed straight for the runway, directly in front of him. Sure enough, it landed within the length of a football field and taxied right past him. Mash tried to get a glimpse of the pilot and swore he saw a white beard.

Mash found a spot where he could sit unseen and watch his surroundings. He did this until well past midnight, when he felt it was time to move spots and find a place to sleep for a few hours. He did not want to be so dead tired that he would not enjoy the air show the following morning. Mash had not noticed any movement for at least an hour. He had especially not noticed any movement for at least a couple of hours in the area of the plane that the white bearded man had landed. Mash decided to chance it and see if any of the doors of the planes were open. He planned to sleep only for two or three hours at the most and be out well before sunrise.

The first few doors he tried were locked. Mash began to think this was a bad idea. The next plane he came to, he could have sworn, was the plane the white bearded man had landed. He tried the door and it opened. He quickly entered the plane and closed the door behind him. The inside of the plane smelled faintly like paint, and the thought puzzled Mash until his eyes found the cockpit. He approached it as one might a holy altar. He sat down in the pilot's chair and gripped the wheel, or stick. Mash noticed the two pedals at his feet. He looked at the instrument panel in front of him and thought he just might pass out with joy. Mash found a headset and put it on. He found the hand microphone and pretended to call the tower. He studied the panel in front of him and thought of all the books he had read about airplanes; all

130

the books his grandma had brought him back from the library. Mash quickly found the airspeed indicator, the artificial horizon, the altimeter, and just below that, the compass. He had a pretty good idea of what they all meant and pretended to speak to his passengers.

"Ladies and gentlemen," he began, "I am preparing the plane for takeoff, and in just a few short minutes, we will be on our way to sunny Jamaica. If you have not put on your seatbelt, I would appreciate it at this time if you would do so. Take a deep breath, relax, and we'll be on our way in just a few minutes."

Mash glanced behind him and seemed to notice for the first time that there were no seats in this small plane. It looked as though the seats had been removed and replaced with a giant rectangular item. Mash could not tell what is was, as it was covered with blankets. So excited about being inside a plane for the first time, he turned back around and forgot about it.

Mash pretended he was taxiing down the runway. He talked to the air traffic controllers in the tower, and got permission for takeoff. Imitating what he knew about takeoffs, he pulled back on the wheel and watched the imaginary landscape below him fade away. Looking once again at the control panel, Mash found the knob which controlled the landing gear, and acted as though he was letting it up.

"Ladies and gentlemen," Mash announced again, "if you will look out of the left side of the aircraft, you will see Stone Mountain. Our flight time this afternoon is three hours. The weather for our flight looks like we are in store for perfect conditions and my computer is telling me Jamaica will be ninety-four degrees and sunny this afternoon. Perfect for playing on the beach and for the surfers on board. Enjoy your flight."

Mash was not the type to let his imagination get the best of him, but on this occasion he did. Once he had landed the plane in fantasy Jamaica, and wished all the passengers a wonderful vacation, he looked at his watch. It was four in the morning! He was not tired, but knew he needed to catch a couple hours of sleep. He decided to use the blanket that was covering the mysterious item in the back of the plane as his bed. Mash pulled some of it under him, and some on top of him, and burrowed in like an underground animal.

Mash's mind raced. He was in an airplane! The trip to Jamaica almost seemed real. He was going to see all kinds of airplanes, in just a few hours, at the air show! Mash could not turn off his brain. It ran around and around for another hour until finally he fell asleep. Mash was *hard* asleep. Drool ran down the side of his face, and his dreams filled with airplanes, of course.

Mash forgot to set the alarm on his watch.

Chapter 25

Bad Santa, also known as Nick, met Juniper at the airport at eight in the morning. Nick had two pump sprayers filled with the chemicals that would turn the outside of the plane sky blue. Once applied, the spray took thirty minutes to take effect. Once it did, the plane would only remain this way for ten minutes. Nick reminded Juniper of this as Juniper nodded, remembering what Nick had told him about it earlier. Juniper was jittery and incredibly excited.

"Did you have a lot of coffee this morning, sir?" Nick asked.

"Not this morning," Juniper answered. "Too excited. This is going to be my masterpiece. Imagine what da Vinci must have felt like while painting the Mona Lisa!"

"OK," Nick said, "just try to be calm so we don't arouse any suspicions. It's already going to look a little weird when we spray the plane with the camouflage stuff."

"What if somebody asks about it?"

"I'll tell them it's holy water and that you are a very superstitious priest."

"That is so wrong," Juniper said with a smile.

Nick wanted to tell Juniper it was nothing compared to what he was about to do, but held his tongue. Juniper *was* his boss.

Nick kept an eye on his watch, and when the time was right, he nodded to Juniper and they headed toward the plane, each carrying a pump sprayer, pumped and ready to go. Nick instructed Juniper to spray one side of the plane as he sprayed the other. No one was near them, and they were quiet as mice. Finished, they stashed the sprayers under another plane.

Without a sound, the two men entered the plane, and Nick cranked it up. Mash moved an inch under the blanket, but did not awake. At this point, the plane could have crashed and he would not have awoken. Nick put the plane in motion and dialed his cell phone.

"What are you doing?" Juniper asked.

"Calling the tower," Nick said with a tricky smile.

"I thought you were supposed to use the headset or something like that."

"You should," Nick answered. "But when you have a friend who works in the tower, and you don't want a record of your flight, you use your cell phone."

"You are a genius," Juniper said.

"Thank you, sir," Nick answered.

A few minutes later, they were in the air.

The force of the takeoff pulled Mash's body into the floor and he woke up. He tried to decide, for a few moments, if he was dreaming or if he was awake. Once he decided he was not dreaming, the harsh reality hit him that the airplane in which he had fallen asleep, had taken off and was in the air. He was, basically, completely under the blanket, but he pulled himself into a tight little ball under the blanket, just in case part of his body or clothes was exposed.

Mash listened and tried not to move. After just a few minutes of listening, he could tell that there were only two men in the plane. He discovered that one of the men was called Nick and the other was Juniper. Mash thought the one named Nick sounded familiar.

"You better get that blanket off the paint and take a look at those controls," Nick said. "My buddy that made it, said it is very simple. There is a safety switch you need to turn off when you are ready, and one button to push when you want the paint to be released. Remember, when you push the button, it will somehow force all one hundred and ten gallons of that paint out in two and a half seconds."

"I remember," Juniper said.

Knowing that the blanket was about to be removed, Mash did not know what to do. He did the only thing he could think of and acted as though he was still asleep.

"Holy cow!" Juniper said as he yanked the blanket off the top of the container holding the paint.

Mash pretended to wake up. "Oh my gosh," he cried, "what is going on? I just needed a place to sleep last night and climbed into this plane. The door was open. I didn't mean to do anything wrong."

The sight of a sleeping kid had startled Juniper and he screamed. Nick looked back to see the kid waking up and was shocked as well to find an unknown passenger.

Mash spilled the beans. "I just wanted to come to the air show," he cried. "I live in the big old stinky city and have never been outside of it and all I wanted was to come out here and go to an air show and see some planes. I came out here last night so I wouldn't miss any of it and had to find a place to sleep so I would be safe. The door to your airplane was open and I am sorry I slept in your plane."

Recovering, Juniper said, "It's OK, buddy. We are just taking a short flight and we will be back at the airport in a few minutes. If you promise not to tell anyone you were on this airplane, we won't tell the police that you broke the law and illegally entered the plane."

Mash, for the moment, bought Juniper's bluff. He pulled his backpack to his chest and pushed himself against the back of the craft. Squeezing the backpack against his chest, he felt the shape of the super powerful taser gun.

The stage was set for Stuart and Emilio's first live performance. The giant set of scissors and the ribbon were set to be used at exactly nine o'clock to officially open the King Cone building. Mr. Henry had everything set up and the biscuits were enormous and Stuart thought they smelled so delicious, he might not be able to play.

"I have seen that look before," Mr. Henry said.

"I'm not nervous," Stuart said.

"My biscuits are taking away your nervousness and making you hungry."

"They sure are," Stuart confessed.

"You play your little show and I'll have a special one all set out for you," Mr. Henry teased. "Best you not eat right before your first show."

"You are probably right about that."

Emilio tapped his watch, and Stuart knew it was time. Stuart stepped up to the microphone and welcomed everyone to the grand opening of the King Cone building. For a little before nine o'clock in the morning, there was actually a pretty big crowd. Stuart thanked them all for coming and announced that some special employees would cut the ribbon at exactly nine, as he and Emilio played their short set.

"Don't forget," Emilio said. "If you mess up, don't stop."

"I know," Stuart answered. "I won't even stop if an elephant runs across the stage."

"Good," Emilio answered, "but I said a giraffe!"

Juniper looked out the window and saw the King Cone building in all its wonder coming into view. The six story, white spiral replica of a soft serve ice cream, sitting atop a gold plated cone, high above all the other buildings in the Atlanta skyline. It was the last time it would ever look this way, he thought.

Mash watched what was going on and recognized a moment too late what was about to happen. As Mash reached into his bag for the taser gun, to shoot Juniper and keep him from painting the King Cone building, he saw Juniper releasing the safety and pushing the button.

Stuart and Emilio's set was just about as perfect as it could be. Stuart had not missed a beat and the big moment was at hand. The special employees opened the

136

giant scissors to cut the ribbon to officially open the building and just as they did, they heard a noise from the sky. Unable to see the camouflaged plane, they only saw a hundred and ten gallons of paint fall perfectly on the six story soft serve ice cream cone. The paint could not have fallen on the cone any better than it did. The chocolate colored paint wrapped, swirled, dripped, and coated the cone, leaving it looking like an ice cream masterpiece.

Juniper looked back at the building and had one moment to bask in the glory of his new masterpiece, before the kid, whom he had forgotten was in the corner, called him.

"I saw that," Mash said. He was holding the taser gun in front of himself, pointing it directly at Juniper's chest.

"Easy, buddy," Juniper said. "Take it easy."

Nick looked back and saw Mash holding the taser gun.

"I brought a little something in case of a people problem," Nick said, reaching under his seat. He pulled out an aluminum bat and instructed Juniper to knock the kid out.

Just as Nick was handing the bat to Juniper, and both men had their hands on it, Mash pulled the trigger on the taser gun. The electrodes shot out of the gun and hit Juniper directly in the center of his chest. Since both men had their hands on the bat, the massive amount of electricity travelled from Juniper's body, through the bat, and into Nick's body. Both men instantly hit the floor. Juniper did a face plant in the back and Nick fell sideways out of the pilot's seat.

The plane seemed to hiccup, but stayed level.

"I'm sorry," Mash yelled. He shook Juniper, but he was unresponsive. Mash shook Nick and Nick opened one eye, half way. "We are going to crash," Mash said.

"Go north," Nick mumbled. "Must land."

137

Mash looked at the compass and discovered they were going south. He slid into the pilot's chair and took hold of the wheel. Ever so carefully, he turned the wheel and watched the compass.

"Stay above two thousand feet," Nick mumbled. His leg twitched and he drooled all over himself and he was out again.

Once Mash was headed north, he checked the altimeter and saw that the longest needle was pointing between two and three. The shorter of the needles was pointing just below five. He held the course and looked at the airspeed indicator. They were travelling one hundred and thirty knots.

Nick sat up.

"Get my cell phone from my front pocket," he commanded.

"You get it," Mash answered.

"I can't feel my arms or my legs, yet," Nick answered.

Mash pulled the phone out of Nick's pocket. Nick instructed him what number to dial and Mash held the phone to his ear after dialing. Nick informed his friend in the tower that they were approaching the airport for their landing. From what he said, Mash could tell that they were ready for them to come in.

"I don't even see the airport," Mash said.

"Turn a little to the east," Nick instructed. Mash did as instructed. "Pull the throttle back a bit and we will start our descent."

"Do I need to push the wheel down?" Mash asked.

"Not yet," Nick answered. "Throttling down will pull us down good enough for now."

As they dropped lower, Mash saw the different runways off in the distance come into view. "I see the runways!" he said. "We need to put the landing gear down." Without instruction, Mash pushed down the landing gear knob.

"How did you know that?" Nick asked.

"I've read a lot of books about this," Mash announced, proudly.

"Alright," Nick said. "We want to get the plane at about ninety knots before we lower the nose. Thank God there is no wind, so just line it up on the runway and slow this baby down. Nice and easy, though.

As they were approaching, Nick could still not feel his arms or legs, but pointed at a knob with the bob of his head for Mash to pull. "Pull that one," Nick instructed.

Doing so, Mash asked, "What was that?"

"It keeps the carburetor from icing up."

"Oh," Mash said. "I must have missed that one in my books."

"You want to be between seventy and eighty knots when we reach the runway. Adjust the throttle as necessary and only push the nose down when the lowering of the throttle doesn't do it for you. When we touch the ground, we will probably bounce a bit, it's cool, just hold it steady and push on top of both of those pedals at your feet."

"Push the top of them?" Mash asked.

"Yes," Nick answered. "The top of the pedals apply the brakes. And when I tell you, I want you to turn off the key."

"OK," Mash said.

Mash held the controls tight, watched his airspeed, kept the plane steady and in the center of the runway, and only bounced once on his landing. The plane slowed to a stop, almost at the same point where they started, and thanks to Nick's friend in the tower, nobody had a clue what had just happened.

"I'll make a deal with you," Nick began, "if you walk out that door and disappear into the crowd, I'll pretend like we never met."

"Deal," Mash said, still too shaken up to think straight.

As Mash grabbed the door to leave, Nick stopped him saying, "Hey kid, you are one heck of a pilot."

Chapter 26

Stuart did not stop playing, as he watched one hundred and ten gallons of chocolate colored paint fall on his brand new multimillion dollar building. He had made a promise and he always kept his promises.

After the set, as Stuart was eating the biscuit Mr. Henry had saved for him, Mr. Henry asked, "Was that planned?"

"It might as well have been."

"What does that mean?" Mr. Henry asked.

"I didn't plan it, but I wish that I had."

"So, let me get this straight," Mr. Henry said. "You didn't have anything to do with all that paint covering your sky-high vanilla ice cream cone?"

"No, I didn't," Stuart assured.

"And you aren't going to call the police?"

"You're right," Stuart said. "I should. I would like to find out who did this, so I can thank them."

Mr. Henry and Stuart laughed, as a piece of biscuit shot out of Stuart's mouth.

"I think I'm gonna need another biscuit," Stuart announced.

"I knew it!" Mr. Henry laughed. "That's why I made you two!"

Juniper finally woke up, and was surprised there were no police cars all around. He just knew after the kid pulled the taser gun on him, that life as he knew it was over. In the milliseconds before the taser electrodes hit him, Juniper vowed never to do this type of art again, if he was not spending the rest of his life in jail. He got lucky and he knew it.

Juniper watched the driveway for cop cars for days, and when he finally was assured he got away with it, he printed one of the many pictures that had graced newspapers worldwide and placed it in his studio where he could see it from his Lazy Boy. *My new and final masterpiece*, he thought.

Junior continued to train Booger and invent new ice cream flavors for Mr. Teca. She actually invented one that a few people other than herself and Mr. Teca would eat—bacon. Everybody loves bacon. Booger would eat a gallon of it if Junior would let him. One time she did. Bad idea. Juniper even tried the bacon ice cream once and admitted that it was pretty darn good. Junior never asked about the last art project and Juniper just acted as though it had never happened. He did not want to admit to her that the nightmare she had of the boy holding the light saber of electricity over him actually came true. She would never remember. Booger was her world now and Juniper had awoken recently to hear her calling, "Bean bag, bean bag, bean bag." When he asked her what it meant, she looked at him like he was a complete moron and said, "It means, sit. Duh! You sit on bean bags, duh!"

As for Mash, he didn't stay too long at the air show. Why look at planes flying around when you can fly one yourself? He never told anybody what happened; he too was pretty good at keeping promises. In return, he had something alive in his heart that would continue beating and never stop. Something he had known from the very beginning, when nobody else believed him. Something he never doubted. Something he would never, ever forget. HE WAS A PILOT!

12322145R00079

Made in the USA
Charleston, SC
27 April 2012